Marjorie in Command

Carolyn Wells

TABLE OF CONTENTS

CHAPTER I
A FAMILY CONFAB

"Well," said Marjorie, "I think it's too perfectly, awfully, horribly dreadful for anything in all this world!"

"I do, too," agreed King. "It's a calamity, and a catastrophe and a cat,—a cata—cataclysm!"

"Of course it is," said Kitty, who was philosophical. "But as it's all settled, and we've got to live through it, we may as well make the best of it."

"The best of it!" grumbled King; "there isn't any best! It's all outrageously horrid, and that's all there is about it! I don't see how we can stand it."

"S'pose we say we just won't stand it," suggested Marjorie; "do you think they'd stay home?"

"No, indeedy!" declared King. "You know as well as I do, the tickets are bought, and everything is arranged for."

"Even us," said Kitty, sadly.

"Yes; even us," repeated her brother. "And how are we arranged for? Left in charge of Larkin! Old Loony Larkin!"

"Hush, King, that's disrespectful," said Marjorie, laughing in spite of herself.

"Well, she is old; and she is Larkin; and I think she's loony!"

"But you mustn't say so, if you do," persisted Marjorie.

"Indeed you mustn't," said Mrs. Maynard, coming into the living room where the three children were holding an indignation meeting. "I'm ashamed of you, King!"

"Aw, Mother, forgive me this once, and I won't ever say such a thing again till next time."

Kingdon sidled up to his mother, and nestled his cheek against hers in such a cajoling way, that Mrs. Maynard smiled, and forbore further reproof just then.

"But, dearies all," she went on, "you mustn't take such an attitude toward Miss Larkin; she's good and kind and will look after you nicely till I return."

"Larkin, Larkin,

  All the time a-barkin',"

chanted King, pinching his mother's lips together, so she couldn't reprimand him.

The whole tale of the Maynard children's tribulations may be told in a few words.

Mrs. Maynard's health was not quite up to its usual standard, and her husband had decided to take her for a short Southern trip. They would be absent from home about six weeks, and

1

Miss Larkin, a friend of Mrs. Maynard's, was to come and take care of the household of four children.

Now, though the little Maynards were perhaps more inclined to mischief than model children ought to be, they were a loving and affectionate little brood, and, moreover, they truly tried to correct their faults as pointed out to them by their parents.

The fundamental principle of Mr. and Mrs. Maynard's training was common-sense, and this, added to deep parental love, made their discipline both wise and kind.

Mrs. Maynard, herself, had some doubts of Miss Larkin's ability to manage the children tactfully, but there was no one else to ask to stay with them, and they could not be left entirely in charge of the servants, trusted and tried though they were.

But it was only for six weeks, anyway, and as Mr. Maynard said, they couldn't become thorough-going reprobates in that short time.

Miss Larkin was delighted with the prospect. A quiet and rather lonely spinster, she welcomed the idea of a stay in a merry, lively home, where she should be the commanding spirit over both children and servants.

And so, it was only the four small Maynards who raised objections. Though they didn't actively dislike Miss Larkin, they felt she was not in sympathy with their childish affairs and they could not know that this arose from ignorance, not unwillingness on her part.

It was a long time since Miss Larkin had been a child, and when she was, she was not like the children of to-day.

She thought she understood young people, but her ideas were old-fashioned, and often quite contradictory to the Maynards' views.

However, as Kitty had said, the matter was settled. Mr. and Mrs. Maynard were going, Miss Larkin was coming, and all they had to do was to accept the situation and make the best of it.

"And perhaps it won't be so bad," said Mother Maynard, as they talked it over. "When Miss Larkin is living here with you, she'll be more chummy and jolly than when she just comes to call or to spend the day."

"I hope so," sighed Marjorie; "you see, it'll be the worst for me. King's a boy, and he won't have to have much to do with her; Kitty doesn't seem to mind her so much, anyway; and, of course Rosy Posy is too little to care. But I shall have to entertain her, and go walking with her, and,—and, oh, Mother, how I shall miss you!"

Marjorie fairly pulled King out of Mrs. Maynard's arms, and flung herself into them, with one of her sudden bursts of demonstrative affection.

"Take me with you, Mothery," she wailed; "oh, do take me with you!"

"Nonsense, Midget," said Mrs. Maynard, knowing it was best to treat the matter lightly; "why, the family would all go to pieces if you weren't here. As you just now implied you're the most important member of the household, and you're needed here to keep all running smoothly in my absence."

This was a new view of things, and Marjorie brightened up considerably.

"Shall I be head of the house, Mother? May I sit at the head of the table?"

Mrs. Maynard took a moment to think this over. Marjorie was only twelve, and she was sometimes a harum-scarum little girl; but, on the other hand, if she felt a sense of importance, she often acted with good sense and judgment beyond her years. At last Mrs. Maynard said:

"Yes, Midget; I believe I will let you sit at the head of the table. Miss Larkin is really a guest, and I think it would be better for you to be hostess in my place. Kingdon will sit in his father's place, and I shall trust you two to uphold the dignity and decorum of the Maynard household."

"Will Miss Larkin like that?" said Marjorie.

"I think so; or I should not consent to the arrangement. Miss Larkin is, I know, more anxious to please you children, than you are to please her. And so, to please me, I want you all to be very good to her. Kind, polite, deferential, considerate, all the things that a host and hostess should be to their guest."

"H'm," said Marjorie, considering; "p'raps she'd better be hostess, and let me be guest."

"No, Mopsy; that matter's settled. You shall be the lady of the house; and Miss Larkin your honored guest for whose pleasure and comfort you must do all you can."

"Pooh," said King, "if she's only company, I don't see why she need come at all."

"In return for your kindness to her, she will do much for you. She will really keep house, in the sense of giving orders, looking after your clothes and mending, and superintending the servants."

"Must we obey her, Mother?"

"Well, that's rather a delicate point, my boy. I hope there'll be no very serious questions of obedience, for I trust you won't want to do anything that Miss Larkin will think she ought to forbid."

"But if she does, must we obey?" persisted Kingdon.

"Hello, hello! What's all this about love, honor, and obey?" cried a voice in the doorway, and the Maynards looked up to see Mr. Maynard smiling at them as he entered the room.

"Oh, Father!" cried Marjorie, making a spring at him; "do come and help us settle these awful questions. Must we obey Miss Larkin, while you and Mother are away?"

"Me 'bey Miss Larky," said Rosy Posy, as she toddled to her father and clasped him round the knees, nearly upsetting that genial gentleman. "Me goody gail; me 'bey Miss Larky booful."

3

"Kit's good at it, too," said King. "So let Kitty and Rosy Posy do the obeying, and Mops and I will count out."

"What direful deeds are you planning, in defiance of Miss Larkin's orders?" asked Mr. Maynard, sitting down, and taking the baby up in his arms.

"Not any," said King; "but I hate to feel that I must do as she says, whether I want to or not."

"But," said his father, "you always do as Mother says, whether you want to, or not."

"Yes, sir; but then, you see, I love Mother."

This simple explanation seemed to please Mr. Maynard, and he said:

"Well, I wouldn't bother much about this obedience matter. I doubt if Miss Larkin lays down very strict laws, anyway. Suppose you take this for a rule. Don't do anything that you think Mother would forbid if she were at home."

"That's ever so much better," said King, with a sigh of relief. "I did hate to be tied to old Larky's apron strings."

"Hold on, King, my boy. Stop right there. Obedience is one thing, respect another. You are, at my orders, to be respectful to Miss Larkin, both in speech and in spirit. Is that understood?"

"Yes, sir," said Kingdon, looking ashamed. "I understand, and I'll obey; but, Father, we always call her Larky."

"But you won't any more. I don't think you realize what bad taste it is, for a child to speak so of an elder person. Call your school friends by nicknames, if you like, but show to grown-ups the civility and respect that good-breeding calls for."

"All right; I'll call her the Honorable Miss Larkin; Dear Madam," and King swept a magnificent bow nearly to the floor, in token of his great respect for the lady.

"But do hurry home as soon as you can," said Marjorie, as she squeezed her father's coat sleeve with one hand, and with the other reached out to grasp a fold of her mother's trailing gown.

"We'll be gone just six weeks, dearie," said Mr. Maynard. "I can't remain away longer than that. And I think that will be long enough to make the roses bloom once more on Mother's wan cheeks." Mrs. Maynard smiled.

"I'm not really ill, Ed," she said; "it's more of a pleasure trip than a health trip, I think. And six weeks will be quite long enough to burden Miss Larkin with these four beautiful but not very manageable children."

"And, oh, Father," cried Marjorie, "there'll be an Ourday while you're gone! What shall we do about that?"

"Bless my stars!" said Mr. Maynard; "so there will. I hadn't thought of that! Shall we give up the trip, Helen?"

"No," said Kitty, who always took things seriously; "we can have two Ourdays together when you come back."

"Bravo, Kitsie!" said her father; "you have a logical head. I think you had better take charge of the family while we're gone."

"I'm not old enough," said Kitty, practically. "But I'll help all I can."

"I know you will," said Mrs. Maynard, caressing her. "And you'll all do the best you can. I know my quartette, and I can trust them to do right,—if they think in time."

"That's just it," said Mr. Maynard, his eyes twinkling. "I expect King or Midget will pull the house down around Miss Larkin's ears, and then excuse themselves by saying they forgot it was mischievous until it was all over."

"All over Miss Larkin, I suppose you mean," said Marjorie, chuckling at her own joke.

"Oho!" laughed Kingdon; "Mopsy's quite a wit, isn't she? Give us another, Midget!"

As he spoke, he affectionately pulled off Marjorie's hair ribbon, and the mop of dark curls that gave her one of her nicknames came tumbling all over her laughing face.

This was a favorite performance of King's, and though it never teased Marjorie, there was, of course, but one reply to it. That was to tweak the end of King's Windsor tie out of its neat bow, and, if possible, out from under his flat round white collar.

But knowing what was coming, King sprang away and around the table before even quick-motioned Midget could catch him. Of course a race ensued. Round the room they went, knocking over a few chairs and light articles of furniture, until King paused and danced maddeningly up and down on one side of the large centre table, while Midget, at the other side, stood alert to spring after him should he run.

"Mopsy, Midget, Midge, just come around the idge!" sang King, as he made a feint of going one way, then another.

But even as he leaned over to smile teasingly in her face, Marjorie made a quick grab across the table, and just gripped the end of his tie enough to untie it.

Then, of course, peace was declared, although a pile of books was knocked off the table, and a small vase upset.

"My dear children," sighed Mrs. Maynard, as Marjorie, flushed but smiling with victory, came back to her mother to have her hair retied, "why do you have to play so,—so emphatically?"

"Why, I just had to catch him, you see," was Midget's plausible explanation, "'cause a hair-ribbon pull-off always means a necktie untie. Doesn't it, King?"

"Yep," agreed her brother, who was adjusting his tie before a mirror, "always. If Miss Larkin pulls off my tie, I shall sure go for her hair-ribbon."

"I believe you would," said Mrs. Maynard; "and the worst of it is, Miss Larkin will be so anxious to entertain and amuse you, that I'm sure she'll try to enter into your childish games. If she does, do try to remember she's a lady and not a member of the Jinks Club."

"She can be a member if she wants to," said King, condescendingly; "only if she is, she must take what she gets."

"Well, she'll be here pretty soon, and I'll warn her," said Mr. Maynard.

"No," said his wife, "she's not coming to-night, after all. I expected her, but she telephoned to-day that she can't come until to-morrow afternoon."

"And we leave to-morrow morning! Why, my dear, that's too bad."

"Yes; I'm sorry, for there are lots of things I want to tell her. I'll write a long note and leave it for her. And, Marjorie, I trust to you to welcome her properly, and in every way act like a gracious hostess."

"I think I'll practise," said Midget, jumping up. "Now, you be Miss Larkin, Father, and I'll be me."

"Very well," said Mr. Maynard, going out to the hall, and coming in again.

"Why, how do you do, Marjorie?" he said, offering his hand in exact imitation but not caricature of Miss Larkin's vivacious manner. Marjorie suppressed a giggle, and gave her hand, as she said:

"How do you do, Miss Larkin? I hope you understand that we're a very bad crowd of children. At least, King and I are. Kit and Rosy are angels."

"Indeed! I thought you were the angelic one."

"Oh, no; Miss Larkin. I'm awful bad; and King is even worse."

"Nothing of the sort," put in King. "I'm bad, I know, but I can't hold a candle to Mops for real lovely mischief."

"You come pretty near it," said his mother, laughing; "and now scamper, all of you, and make yourselves tidy for dinner."

"Good-by, Miss Larkin," said Marjorie, again shaking hands with her father. "You can't say you haven't been warned!"

"They'll lead the poor girl a dance," said Mrs. Maynard, as she watched the four romp out of the room and up the stairs.

"Oh, it will do her good," replied Mr. Maynard. "And it will do them good too. Even if there are scenes, it will all be a new experience for Miss Larkin, and a shaking up will do her no harm. As to the children, they'll live through it, and if they have some little troubles, it will help to develop their characters. And as for us, Helen, we'll have a good vacation, and come home refreshed and strong to set right anything that has gone wrong in our absence."

"Very well," said Mrs. Maynard, agreeing, as she usually did, with her clever, sensible husband.

CHAPTER II
A FLORAL WELCOME
Breakfast next morning was not the gay, cheery feast it usually was.

Mrs. Maynard came to the table with her hat on, and the children seemed suddenly to realize afresh that their mother was going away.

"Oh," said Marjorie, "I wish I could go to sleep for six weeks, and then wake up the day you come home again."

"Oh, you have that farewell feeling now," said Mr. Maynard; "but after we're really gone, and you find out what fun it is to have no one to rule over you, you'll begin to wish we would stay six months instead of six weeks." Marjorie cast a look of reproach at her father.

"Not much!" she said, emphatically. "I wish you'd only stay six days, or six hours."

"Or six minutes," added Kitty. But at last the melancholy meal was over, and the good-bys really began.

"Cut it short," said Mr. Maynard, fearing the grief of the emotional children would affect his wife's nerves.

They clung alternately to either parent, now bewailing the coming separation, and again cheering up as Mr. Maynard made delightful promises of sending back letters, postcards, pictures and gifts from every stopping-place on their journey.

"And be very good to Miss Larkin," said Mrs. Maynard, by way of final injunction. "Cheer her up if she is lonely, and then you'll forget that you're lonely yourselves." This was a novel idea.

"Oho!" said King, "I guess she'd better cheer us up."

"Oh, the four of you can cheer each other," said Mr. Maynard. "Come, Helen, the carriage is waiting—Good-by for the last time, chickadees. Now, brace up, and let your mother go away with a memory of four smiling faces."

This was a pretty big order, but the Maynard children were made of pretty good stuff after all, and in response to their father's request they did show four smiling, though tearful faces, as Mrs. Maynard waved a good-by from the carriage window. But as the carriage passed through the gate and was lost to their sight, the four turned back to the house with doleful countenances indeed.

Rosy Posy recovered first, and at an invitation from Nurse to come and cut paper-dolls, she went off smiling in her usual happy fashion. Not so the others.

Kitty threw herself on the sofa and burying her face in a pillow sobbed as if her heart would break.

This nearly unnerved King, who, being a boy, was specially determined not to cry.

7

"Let up, Kit," he said, with a sort of tender gruffness in his tone. "If you don't you'll have us all at it. I say, Mops, let's play something."

"Don't feel like it," said Marjorie, who was digging at her eyes with a wet ball of a handkerchief.

It was Saturday, so they couldn't go to school, and there really seemed to be nothing to do.

But reaction is bound to come, and after a time, Kitty's sobs grew less frequent and less violent; King managed to keep his mouth up at the corners; and Marjorie shook out her wet handkerchief and hung it over a chair-back with some slight feeling of interest.

"I think," Midget began, "that the nicest thing to do this morning would be something that Mother would like to have us do. Something special, I mean."

"Such as what?" asked Kitty, between two of those choking after-sobs that follow a hard crying-spell.

"I don't know, exactly. Can't you think of something, King? Maybe something for Miss Larkin."

"I'll tell you," said King; "let's put flowers in her room! Mother would like us to do that."

"All right," said Midget, but without enthusiasm; "only I meant something bigger. Something that would take us all the morning. We could put a bouquet of flowers up there in five minutes."

"But I don't mean just a bouquet," explained King. "I mean a lot of flowers—decorate it all up, you know." Marjorie brightened, and Kitty displayed a cordial interest.

"Wreaths and garlands," went on King, drawing on his imagination, "and a 'Welcome' in big letters."

"Fine!" cried Kitty, who loved to decorate; "and festoons and streamers and flags."

"All right, come on!" said Midget. "Let's give her a rousing good welcome. It'll please her, and it will please Mother when we tell her."

"But what shall we make our wreaths and garlands of?" asked Kitty, who was always the first to see the practical side.

"That's so," said King, "there isn't a flower in the garden." As it was only the second week in March, not many flowers could be expected to be in bloom.

"Never mind," said Marjorie, her ingenuity coming to the rescue, "there's lots of evergreen and laurel leaves to make wreaths and things, and we can make paper flowers. Pink tissue paper roses are lovely."

"So they are," agreed Kitty. "'Deed we will have enough to do to fill up the morning. You go and cut a lot of greens, King, and Mopsy and I will begin on the flowers."

8

"Haven't any pink paper," said Midget. "Let's all go downtown and get that first, and then we can get some ice cream soda at the same time."

"That's a go!" cried King. "Hurry up, girls."

In ten minutes the three were into their hats and coats, and arm in arm started for the village drug shop.

In this convenient store, they found pink paper and equally pink ice cream soda. Having despatched the latter with just enough procrastination to appreciate its exquisite flavor and texture, they took their roll of tissue paper and hastened home.

Then Marjorie and Kitty went to work in earnest, and it is astonishing how fast pink paper roses can grow under skilful little fingers. Their method was a simple one. A strip of paper was cut, about twelve inches long and two inches wide. This was folded in eight sections, and the folded tops cut in one round scallop. Thus, the paper when unfolded, showed eight large scallops. These were the rose petals, and were deftly curled a trifle at the edges, by the use of an ivory paper-knife. Then the strip was very loosely rolled round itself, the pretty petals touched into place, the stem end pinched up tight and wound with a bit of wire, which also formed a stem.

Midge and Kitty had made these before, and were adept in the art.

So when King came in, they had a good-sized waste-basket filled with their flowers.

King brought not only evergreens, and laurel sprays, but some trailing vines that had kept green through the winter's frost.

"There!" he said, as he deposited his burden on the floor; "I guess that will decorate Larky's room—I mean the Honorable Miss Larkin's room—just about right. Jiminy, what a lot of flowers!"

"Yes, aren't they fine!" agreed Marjorie. "We have enough now, Kit, let's take 'em up."

Upstairs they went, to the pretty guest room that had been appointed for Miss Larkin's use, during her stay with the Maynards. Many hands make light work, and soon the room was transformed.

From a dainty, well-appointed chamber, it changed to the appearance of a holiday bazaar of some sort.

Garlands of greens, stuck full of pink roses, wreathed the mirrors and pictures. Wreaths or nosegays were pinned to the lace curtains, tied to the brass bedposts, and set around on bureau, tables, mantel, and wherever a place could be found. The Maynard children had no notion of moderation, and with them, to do anything at all, usually meant to overdo it, unless restrained by older heads and hands.

"I think streamers are pretty," said Marjorie. "Let's tie our best sashes on these big bouquets."

"Oh, yes," said Kitty, "and some hair-ribbons, too."

A hasty visit to their bedroom resulted in many ribbons and sashes, which were soon fluttering gracefully from wreaths, bedposts, and chair-backs.

"We must have a 'Welcome' somewhere," said King, as he stood, with his hands in his pockets, admiring the results of their labors.

"There's a great big 'Welcome' sign, up in the attic," said Kitty; "the one we had for a transparency when the Governor came, you know."

"Oh, I know!" cried King. "That big white muslin thing, with black letters. I'll get it."

He raced away to the attic, and soon came back with the big painted sign.

As it was about ten feet long, it was nearly unmanageable, but at last they managed to fasten it up above the mantel, and it surely gave evidence of a hearty welcome to the coming guest.

"I found this in the attic, too," said King, unrolling a smaller strip of muslin.

This bore the legend "We Mourn Our Loss," and had been used many years before, beneath the portrait of a martyred President.

"I thought," he explained, "that it seemed too bad to make such a hullabaloo over Miss Larkin, and make no reference to Father and Mother."

"Oh, I think so, too," cried Marjorie. "It will be lovely to put this up in memory of them. Shall we drape it in black?"

"No, you goose!" said King. "They aren't dead! We'll put a little flag at each corner, like a Bon Voyage thing, or whatever you call it."

"Oh, yes; like the pillow Mother sent to Miss Barstow when she went to Europe. That had a flag in each corner, and Bon Voyage right across it, cattycorner. What does Bon Voyage mean, anyway?"

"It means 'hope you have a good time,'" said Kitty; "and I'm sure we hope Father and Mother will have a good time."

"Yes, I know," said Midget, "but what has that got to do with Miss Larkin?"

"Oh, well, we may as well do our decorating all in one room," said sensible Kitty. "Come on, let's hurry up and finish; I'm awful tired, and hungry, too."

"So'm I," said both the others, and they finished up their decorating in short order.

"Sarah," called Marjorie, at last, to the good-natured and long-suffering waitress, "won't you please come and clear away this mess; we've finished our work."

"For goodness' sake, Miss Marjorie!" exclaimed Sarah, as she saw the guest room; "now, why did you do this? Your mother told me to put this room tidy for the lady, and I did, and now you've gone and cluttered it all up."

10

"You're mistaken, Sarah," said King. "We've decorated it in honor of the lady that's coming. Now, you just take away the stuff on the floor, and sweep up a bit, and straighten the chairs, and smooth over the bed, and the room will look lovely."

"And perhaps you'd better put on fresh pillow-shams," added Marjorie; "somehow those got all crumpled. And we broke the lampshade. Can't you get one out of Mother's room to replace it?"

"Oh, yes," said Sarah, half laughing, half grumbling; "of course I can do the room all over. It needs a thorough cleaning after all this mess."

"Well, thorough-clean it, then," said Marjorie, patting Sarah's arm. "But don't touch our decorations! They're to assure the lady of our welcome."

"I'll not touch 'em, Miss Marjorie; but any lady'd get the nightmare to sleep in such a jungle as this."

"It is like a jungle, isn't it?" said King. "I didn't think of that before. Maybe Miss Larkin will think we mean she's a wild beast."

"No," said Kitty, with her usual air of settling a question. "It's lovely, all of it. You just tidy up, Sarah, and it will be all right, and Miss Larkin will adore it. Is luncheon ready?"

"Almost, Miss Kitty. It will be by when you're ready yourselves."

The children gave one more admiring glance at their decorations, and then ran away to get ready for luncheon.

"What time is she coming?" asked Kitty, as she and Midge tied each other's hair-ribbons.

"I don't know, exactly. About four, Mother thought. She told me to show her to her room, and ask her if she'd like tea sent up."

"Doesn't it make you feel grown up to do things like that?" asked Kitty, looking at her older sister with admiring eyes.

"Yes—sort of. But I forget it right away again, and feel little-girlish. Come on, Kits, are you ready?"

Luncheon was great fun. Marjorie at one end of the table, and King at the other, felt a wonderful sense of dignity and responsibility. Kitty and Rosy seemed to them very young and childish.

"Will you have some cold beef, Marjorie," said King, "or a little of the omelet?"

"Both, thank you," replied Midget, "and a lot of each."

"Ho! that doesn't sound like Mother," said King, grinning.

"I don't care," said Marjorie. "Just because I sit in Mother's place, I'm not going to eat as little as she does! I'd starve to death."

"All right, sister, you shall have all you want," and King gave Sarah a well-filled plate for Midget's delectation.

"Isn't it fun to be alone?" said Kitty, and then added hastily: "I don't mean without Mother and Father, I mean without Miss Larkin."

"Yes," agreed Marjorie. "I do feel glad that she didn't come this morning, and we can lunch alone. It's sort of like a party."

"I wish it was a party," said Kitty, "'cause then we'd have ice cream."

"P'raps we'll have ice cream a lot, when Miss Larkin gets here," said Marjorie. "Mother left a letter for her, and it says for her to order everything nice to eat."

"Then I'm glad she's coming," declared Kitty, who loved good things to eat.

After luncheon the hours dragged a little. The house seemed empty and forlorn, and the children didn't know exactly what to do.

"Why don't you go over to see Delight?" Kitty asked of her sister; "and then, I'll go to see Dorothy."

"I don't feel like it," answered Midget. "I feel all sort of lost, and I don't want Delight, or anybody else—except Mother."

"Huh!" said King, "squealing already! Chuck it, Mops. Come on outdoors and play tag."

King's suggestion proved a good one, for somehow a game of tag in the cool, bracing, outdoor air did them all good, and when at last it was time to dress for afternoon, and to receive Miss Larkin, it was a smiling group of children who awaited the coming guest.

CHAPTER III
THE LADY ARRIVES
It was about four o'clock when Miss Larkin arrived. Mindful of their newly-acquired dignity, the children awaited her in the drawing-room.

But when Sarah opened the hall door for the guest, a great commotion was heard.

"Yes," said Miss Larkin's high, shrill voice; "that trunk must be put in my bedroom; also these two suit-cases, and this hold-all. Oh, yes, and this travelling-bag. That other trunk may be put in your trunk-room if you have one—or attic, if you haven't. I sha'n't want it for several weeks yet. This basket, take to the kitchen—be careful with it—and these other things you may put anywhere for the present. Where are the babies? the dear babies?"

"Oh, King, she's fairly moving in!" said Marjorie, in a whisper, as she saw James, the coachman, carrying a rocking-chair through the hall, and Sarah's arms piled with wraps and bundles.

But encumbered as she was, Sarah managed to usher Miss Larkin into the drawing-room.

"Oh, here you are, little dears!" exclaimed the visitor, as she rushed rapidly from one to another, and, disregarding their polite curtseys, kissed each child heartily on the cheek. "My poor, orphaned babies! Don't grieve for your parents. I will be to you all that they could be. Come to me with your little troubles. I will soothe and comfort you."

"Yes, Miss Larkin," said Marjorie, rather bewildered by this flood of conversation. "Mother said you would look after us. And now, would you like to go to your room, and have some tea sent up?"

Miss Larkin stared at her in amazement.

"Tea!" she said; "why, bless my soul, child, yes, of course, I should like tea; but I supposed I should order it myself. What do you know about tea, little one?"

It suddenly dawned on Marjorie that Miss Larkin looked upon them all as helpless infants, and had no realization that they were not all of Rosy Posy's age. She suppressed a smile, and said:

"Why, Mother said you were to have it when you came; either down here, or in your room, as you wish."

Still Miss Larkin seemed unable to take it in.

"Yes, dear," she said, "I'll have it upstairs, whilst I rest, and unpack some of my things. But I came here to be housekeeper for you, not to have you look after me."

"All right, Miss Larkin," said King, pleasantly. "You can housekeep all you like. Midget isn't very good at it. Now, if you're going to your room, we'll all go, too, and see how you like it."

"Ess, Miss Larky," put in Rosy Posy. "Come on—see booful f'owers and pitty welcome flag."

"What's a welcome flag?" inquired Miss Larkin, but her question was not answered, as the children were already leading the way upstairs.

They were followed by two or three of the servants, who were carrying up the astonishing amount of luggage which the guest had brought. Marjorie thought they had never had a visitor with so many bags and boxes; but then their visitors didn't often stay so long as six weeks.

The children pranced into the room first, and waited in delighted impatience to hear Miss Larkin's words of approval.

"What are you doing here?" she inquired, pleasantly. "Having a fair of some sort? Is this your playroom?"

"No, Miss Larkin," explained Marjorie. "This is your room. We decorated it on purpose for you. We want you to feel welcome."

The lady looked around at the bewildering array of greens and pink flowers.

It was a trying moment, for Miss Larkin's tastes were inclined toward the Puritanical, and she liked a large room almost bare of furniture, and scrupulously prim and tidy.

Had she followed her inclinations, she would have said to Sarah, "Sweep all this rubbish out"; but as she saw the children's expectant faces, evidently waiting for her to express her appreciation, her tactfulness served her just in time.

"For me!" she exclaimed; "you did all this for me! Why, you dear, dear children!"

They capered round her in glee. It was a success, then, after all.

"Yes," cried Marjorie, "it's all for you, and we're so glad you like it. That is, the 'Welcome' is for you; the other sign, with the flags on it, is for Mother and Father—in their memory, you know."

"Yes," said Miss Larkin, though her lips were twitching, "yes, I know."

"The ribbons, of course, we will take back," explained careful Kitty; "for they're our sashes and hair-ribbons. But they can stay all the time you're here—unless we need some of them—and the flowers you can take home with you, if you like. They're only paper, you see."

"Of course," said Miss Larkin. "One couldn't expect real roses at this time of year, and anyway paper ones are so much more lasting."

"Yes, and they smell good, too," said Marjorie, "for I sprayed them with the cologne atomizer."

"Where are you going to put all your things?" asked Kingdon, with interest, as the servants continued to bring in luggage.

"Well," said Miss Larkin, thoughtfully, "I don't know. I brought this rocking-chair, because I never go anywhere without it. It's my favorite chair. But I thought we could take out one of your chairs to make room for it. I don't like much furniture in my room."

"Of course," said Marjorie, politely. "King, won't you put that wicker rocker in Mother's room? Then Miss Larkin's chair can be by the window."

"Good boy," said the visitor, with an approving smile, as King took away the wicker chair.

"And now," she went on, as he returned, "if you'll just take away also that small table, and those two chairs over there, and that sewing-screen, and that large waste-basket, and that tabouret and jardiniere, I'll be much obliged."

"Whew!" said King; "I think I'll ask Thomas to come up and help me. Are you sure you want all those taken out, Miss Larkin?"

"Yes, child. The room is too full of useless furniture. I can't stand it."

"Well, Miss Larkin," said Marjorie, "I'm sure Mother would like you to have things just as you want them. But I don't believe we children can help you fix them. I think we'd better go downstairs and be out of your way. Then you tell Sarah and Thomas what you want, and they'll do it."

"Very well," said Miss Larkin, with a preoccupied air. She was trying her rocking-chair as she spoke, now at one window and now at another, and seemed scarcely to hear Marjorie's words.

14

Just then, Sarah appeared with the tea-tray, and so Midget told her to await Miss Larkin's orders, and to call Thomas, if necessary, to help her move the furniture.

Then the four children went downstairs, and after giving Rosamond over to the care of Nurse Nannie, they held a council of war.

"She's crazy," said Marjorie, with an air of deep conviction.

"I knew it!" declared King. "You know I called her Loony Larky. You needn't frown at me, Midge; I'm not calling her that now. I'm just reminding you."

"Well, I believe she is. Did you ever hear of a guest cutting up so?"

"I don't believe she liked the decorations," said Kitty, thoughtfully.

"She said she did," observed King.

"Yes; but that was just so she wouldn't hurt our feelings," went on Kitty. "I saw her look when she first got into the room, and I thought she looked disgusted. Then, to be nice to us, she said they were lovely."

"Then she's deceitful," said Marjorie, "and that's a horrid thing to be."

"'Most always it is," argued patient Kitty; "but it's sometimes 'scusable when you do it to be polite. She couldn't very well tell us she hated our greens and roses—but I know she did."

"I know it, too," said King, gloomily. "We had all that trouble for nothing."

"Well," said Marjorie, after thinking a moment; "even if she didn't like the welcome and garlands, she must have 'preciated the trouble we took, and she must have understood that we meant to please her."

"'Course she did," said Kitty, "and that's why she seemed pleased about it. Now, I think, we'd better go up and tell her that if she wants to, she can have all that stuff carted out."

"Oh, Kit!" cried Midge, reproachfully. "It's so pretty, and we worked so hard over it."

"I know it, Mops, but if she doesn't want it there, it's a shame for her to have to have it."

"You're right, old Kitsie," said King; "you're right quite sometimes often. Mops, she is right. Now let's go up and inform the Larky lady—I mean Larkin lady, that we won't feel hurt if she makes a bonfire of our decorations in her honor."

"I shall," said Marjorie, pouting a little.

"Oh, pshaw, Mops; don't be a silly. A nice hostess you are, if you make a guest sleep in a jungle, when she likes a plain, bare room."

Marjorie's brow cleared. A sense of responsibility always called out her better nature, and she agreed to go with the others to see Miss Larkin. Upstairs they tramped, King between his two sisters, and as the Maynards rarely did anything quietly, they sounded like a small army pounding up the steps.

"What is the matter?" exclaimed Miss Larkin, flying to her door as they approached.

"Why, we came to tell you," began Marjorie, somewhat out of breath, "that—that———"

"That if you'd rather not have that racket of 'Welcome' stuff in your room, you can pitch it out," continued King.

"Just tell Thomas," went on Kitty, in her soft, cooing way, "and he'll carry it all away for you."

"But why shouldn't I like it?" said Miss Larkin, who hadn't quite grasped the rapid speech of the children.

"Oh, 'cause it is trumpery," said King. "And we think that you just hate it———"

"And that you said it was nice, so not to 'fend us," went on Kitty, "and so, we'll freely forgive you if you don't want it. But we do want our ribbons back."

"And we may as well keep the 'Welcome' and the mournful signs," added Marjorie; "for you see, our next guest might be of a more—more gay and festive nature."

"Oh, I'm gay and festive," said Miss Larkin, with her funny little giggle, which somehow always irritated the children; "but since you insist, I believe I will have these greens taken away. The scent of evergreens is a little overpowering to my delicate nerves. I shouldn't have dreamed of suggesting it, but since you have done so—ah, may I ring for Thomas at once?"

Sarah answered Miss Larkin's bell, and Thomas was sent for.

Then the lady seemed to forget all about the children, and returned to her tea and bread-and-butter.

Feeling themselves dismissed, they went downstairs again.

"Goodness, gracious, sakes alive!" said King, slowly; "have we got to live six weeks with that?"

"Don't be disrespectful," said Marjorie, remembering her father's words, "but I do think she's just about the worst ever."

"We've got to have her here," said Kitty, "so we may as well make the best of it."

"Oh, Kittums," groaned King, "you'd make the best of a lame caterpillar, I do believe."

"Well, you might as well," protested Kitty, stoutly. She was used to being chaffed about her optimism, but still persisted in it, because it was innate with her.

"All right," said King, "let's forget it. What do you say to 'Still Pond; no moving'?"

16

This was a game that greatly belied its name, for though supposed to be played in silence, it always developed into a noisy romp.

But for this very reason it was a favorite with the Maynard children, and by way of cheering their flagging spirits, they now entered into it with unusual zest.

"Do you s'pose Miss Larkin is playing this same game with Thomas and Sarah?" asked Marjorie, as during a lull in their own game they heard as much, if not more noise in the room above.

"'Spect she's still moving furniture," said King, after listening a moment. "Hope she doesn't take a fancy to my new chiffonier."

"We ought to have told her what time dinner is," said Marjorie.

"You're a gay old hostess, aren't you, Mops?" teased her brother.

But Kitty said, "Oh, she'll ask Sarah. Don't let's think any more about her till dinner time."

This was good advice, and was promptly acted upon.

And so it was half-past six before the young Maynards saw their guest again.

Miss Larkin had asked the dinner hour of Sarah, and promptly to the minute she came downstairs, attired in a black silk dress, quite stiff with jet ornaments.

"I am your guest to-night, my dears," she said, as she patted each one's head in turn; "but to-morrow I shall myself take up the reins of government, and all household cares. I have a letter, left for me by your dear mother, in which she bids me do just as I think best in all matters. She tells me to order such things as I wish, and to command the servants as I choose. I'm sure I need not tell you I shall do my best to make you all comfortable and happy."

Miss Larkin beamed so pleasantly on the children, that it was impossible not to respond, so they all smiled back at her, while Marjorie said, "I'm sure you will, Miss Larkin."

"And now," the lady went on, "I have here a little gift for each of you. I brought them to show my love and affection for you all."

Then she gave to each of the quartette a small box, and sat beaming benignantly as the children tore open the wrappings.

Cries of delight followed, for the gifts were lovely, indeed.

Marjorie's was a narrow gold bangle, set all round with tiny half-pearls.

Kitty's was a gold ring, with a turquoise setting.

King's, a pair of pretty sleeve-links, and Rosy Posy's a pair of little gold yoke pins.

"Oh, Miss Larkin!" exclaimed Marjorie, over-whelmed by the beauty and unexpectedness of these gifts.

"It's just like Christmas," declared King, and Kitty, too pleased for words, went slowly up to Miss Larkin and kissed her.

The baby was scarcely old enough to be really appreciative, but the other three were delighted with their presents, and said so with enthusiasm.

"I'm glad you like them," said Miss Larkin, "and now let us go to dinner."

Marjorie felt a little shy as she took her place at the head of the table, and she asked Miss Larkin if she wished to sit there.

"No, my dear; your mother wrote in her note that she wished you to have that seat. I shall, of course, exercise a supervision over your manners, and tell you wherein I think they may be improved."

This speech made Marjorie feel decidedly embarrassed, and she wondered why she liked Miss Larkin one minute and didn't like her the next.

Then she smiled to herself as she realized that she liked her when she presented pearl bracelets, and didn't like her when she proposed discipline!

This was a fine state of affairs, indeed!

And so compunctious did it make Marjorie feel, that she said, "I hope you will correct me, when I need it, Miss Larkin; for my manners are not very good."

King and Kitty stared at this. What had come over wilful, headstrong Midget to make her talk like that?

But Miss Larkin only smiled pleasantly, and made no comment on Marjorie's manners as a hostess, all through dinner.

As the two sisters were going to bed that night, Kitty said:

"I can't make her out. I think she's real nice, and then the next minute she does something so queer, I don't know what to make of it."

"I think she's what they call eccentric," said Marjorie. "And I do believe if we let her alone a good deal, she'll let us alone. She seems awfully wrapped up in her own affairs. If she doesn't interfere too much, I think we'll get along all right. But I wish Mother was home."

"So do I. Oh, Mops, there isn't one day gone yet! Out of forty-two!"

"Well, skip into bed; the time flies faster when you're asleep."

"So it does," agreed Kitty; "good-night."

CHAPTER IV
THE IDES OF MARCH
Somehow, the days managed to follow each other much at their usual rate of speed. Life held a great variety of interests for the little Maynards, and though at times they greatly missed their parents, yet at other times they were gaily absorbed in their work or play, and were happy

and bright as usual. Miss Larkin proved to be rather an uncertain quantity. Sometimes she ruled the household with a rod of iron, laying down laws and issuing commands with great austerity. And then, again, she would seem to forget all about the Maynards and become absorbed in her own affairs, even neglecting to give orders for dinner!

But the children didn't care. So long as she left them free to pursue their own important occupations, she was welcome to amuse herself in any way she chose. And with good-natured, large-hearted Ellen in charge of the kitchen, there was no danger of any one going hungry for long.

Instead of going to school, as King and Kitty did, Marjorie went every day across the street to Delight Spencer's, where Miss Hart, Delight's governess, taught both girls. Miss Hart's methods of teaching were unusual, but exceedingly pleasant.

Often the girls had no idea as to what lessons would be taught until they came to the schoolroom.

And so, as Marjorie and Delight, with their arms about each other, came into Miss Hart's presence one morning, they saw on the schoolroom wall a placard bearing this legend:

"The Ides of March are come."

"What does that mean, Miss Hart?" asked Marjorie, always interested by something she did not understand.

"That's our subject for to-day," said Miss Hart, smiling. "Have you no idea what it means?"

"Not the leastest bit," replied Marjorie. "Have you, Delight?"

"No," said Delight, shaking her golden head very positively. "Unless you meant ideas, Miss Hart, and spelled it wrong on purpose."

"No," said Miss Hart, smiling; "that's not the idea at all. Well, girlies, to begin with, here's a little present for each of you."

Then Miss Hart handed them each a thin, flat volume, which proved to be a pretty edition of Shakespeare's "Julius Cæsar."

Opening it, Marjorie was glad to see it contained many pictures, besides a lot of rather grown-up looking reading.

"To begin with," said Miss Hart, "the Ides of March are really come. To-day is the fifteenth, which, as I will explain to you, is what was called in the Roman Calendar, the Ides."

Then Miss Hart went on to explain how the Roman Calendar was originally made up, and how it has been modified for our present use, all of which, described in her interesting way, proved a pleasant lesson, and one which the girls always remembered.

"Now," Miss Hart went on, "we come to the consideration of our little book, which is one of Shakespeare's greatest and most famous plays. In the very beginning of it, as you may see, on this page, a soothsayer bids Cæsar 'Beware the Ides of March.' Cæsar paid little attention to him at the time, but, as we will learn from our study of the play, the Ides of March was indeed a dread day for Cæsar, for on that day he was cruelly stabbed and killed."

"Oh!" cried Marjorie, who loved tragic tales, "may we read about it now?"

"Yes; but first I will tell you a little of Julius Cæsar, himself."

Miss Hart then gave a short description of Cæsar and his time, and then they again turned to their books.

"Before we begin to read," she said, "note these lines in the first scene of Act II. You see, Brutus says, 'Is not to-morrow the Ides of March?' And he sends a boy to look in the Calendar and find out. What does the boy say when he returns?"

Quick-sighted Marjorie had already looked up this, and read the boy's answer, "Sir, March is wasted fifteen days."

"So you see," went on Miss Hart, "it was the eve of the fatal day. And now turn to the first line of Act III."

Delight read this aloud: "The Ides of March are come."

"Yes, Cæsar said that himself, remembering the soothsayer's warning."

"Did he really say it, Miss Hart?"

"Well, you see, Delight, Shakespeare's plays, though founded on historical facts, are not really history. And, then, we must remember that this play was written sixteen hundred years after the death of Cæsar, and though true, in part, to history and tradition, much of it is Shakespeare's own fancy and imagination. As we study it we must try to appreciate his wonderful command of thought and language."

"What is a soothsayer, Miss Hart?" asked Marjorie, who was already devouring the first pages with her eager eyes.

Then Miss Hart explained all about the soothsayers and fortune-tellers of ancient times; and how, at that time, people put faith in the prognostications of witches and astrologers, which facts were utilized by Shakespeare to lend picturesqueness and mystery to his plays. So enthralled were the two girls with the descriptions of wizardry and soothsaying, and so many questions did they ask of Miss Hart, that the morning was gone before they had time to begin the actual reading of the play.

"But I didn't expect to read it to-day," said Miss Hart, smiling at Marjorie's dismay when she found it was half-past twelve. "This is our literature class, and if we devote about one day a week to it, we'll get through the play by vacation time, and next term we'll take up another."

"But I can read it at home, can't I?" asked Midget.

"Yes, if you like. But there will be much that you can't understand. Our study of it will branch out into Roman history in general, and the manners and customs of ancient Rome, as well as the art and architecture."

"Oh, Miss Hart," exclaimed Marjorie, "it is such fun to come to school to you. It's so different from regular school-work."

"I'm glad you like it, dear, and I'm quite sure you're learning as much and as useful knowledge as is taught in the average school."

"I know we are," said Midget, with conviction. "I've been to regular school, and I know all about it."

With her precious Shakespeare book clasped tightly in her arm, Marjorie ran home to luncheon.

"Oh, Miss Larkin," she exclaimed, as they all sat at table, "did you ever read Shakespeare's 'Julius Cæsar'?"

"Not all of it," said Miss Larkin. "I don't care much for his historical plays. I think they're heavy and uninteresting."

"Oh, do you? Why, I don't see how anything could be more interesting than 'Julius Cæsar.' I'm going to read it right straight through this afternoon."

"Me, too," said King. "Let me read with you, Midgie, won't you?"

"Me, too," said Rosy Posy; "me wead wiv Middy, too."

"Count me out," said Kitty. "I'm going over to Dorothy's this afternoon."

And so, as baby Rosamond's request was not taken seriously, King and Marjorie settled themselves comfortably on the big divan in the living-room, to enjoy their new-found treasure.

"Whew! it's great stuff, isn't it, Midget?" cried King, as they read rapidly on, skipping what they couldn't understand, but getting the gist of the plot.

"Fine!" agreed Marjorie, as, with shining eyes and tumbled hair, she galloped through the printed pages. "But what a shame to stab poor old Cæsar just because it was the fifteenth of March!"

"Pooh! that wasn't the only reason. And, anyway, if they hadn't stabbed him there wouldn't have been any play at all!"

"That's so. Unless they had stabbed somebody else. I say, King, let's play it ourselves."

"'Course we will. It's good to have a new play—I'm tired of Indians every time. Shall we play it now?"

"Yep; Kitty'll be home at five o'clock, and it's 'most five now. See the pictures; they all wear sheets."

"They're not really sheets, they're tunics or togars, or whatever you call 'em."

"Toggas, I guess you say."

"Yes; just like toggery. Well, you get some sheets, and I'll make paper soldier caps for helmets."

"That will do for to-day; but we'll play it better some other day, and make good helmets with gilt paper or something."

"All right; skip for the sheets."

Marjorie flew for the sheets, and came back from the linen closet with several. She brought also her Roman sash, which, she felt sure, would add a fine touch of local color.

Kitty had arrived in the meantime, and though she had not read the play, she was quite ready to take her part, and skimming over the book hastily, announced:

"I'll be Brutus; I think he's the gayest one."

"All right," said King; "who'll be Cæsar?"

"Let Rosy Posy be Cæsar," said Marjorie. "He doesn't do anything but get killed. So that will be easy for her."

The baby was called down from the nursery, and expressed great willingness to be killed in the great cause.

As most of the Maynards' games included a killing of some sort, they were all used to it, and it held no horrors for them.

King was to be Antony, and Marjorie, Cassius, but they were also to assume other parts when necessity arose.

It was, of course, only an initial performance, for the Maynards, when they liked a new game, kept it up day after day, until they tired of it. Much time was spent in adjusting their togas, and though all looked well in the flowing white drapery, they agreed that Rosy Posy, bundled up in a crib sheet, and with a gilt paper crown on her curly head, was easily the noblest Roman of them all.

The first part of the play went well, the actors snatching a glance now and then at the book, to get a high-sounding phrase to declaim.

Marjorie's favorite was, "Help! ho! They murder Cæsar!" which she called out at intervals, long before it was time for the fatal thrust.

Kitty liked the line, "The clock hath stricken three!" and used it frequently, changing the time to suit the moment.

King thundered out, "Yond Cassius hath a lean and hungry look!" which, when spoken at plump Marjorie, savored of the humorous.

However, the play went blithely on, each speaking in turn their own words or Shakespeare's, as the impulse moved them.

"Hey, Casca," said Kitty, "what hath chanced to-day, that Cæsar looks so sad?"

As Rosy Posy was at that moment rolling about in shouts of laughter, the remark missed its point, but nobody cared.

"Beware the Ides of March!" roared Marjorie to the giggling Cæsar, and Kitty chimed in:

"Ay; the clock hath stricken twenty minutes to six! Speak! strike! redress!"

"Does that mean to dress over again?" asked King. "'Cause we haven't time now. We've just about time to kill Cæsar before dinner."

"Come on, then," said Marjorie; "we'll have the killing scene now. King, bring in the umbrella-stand for Pompey's pillar."

"Yes," said King, "and we'll put a sofa-pillar down here by it for Cæsar to tumble onto, when he's stabbed enough. Catch on, Rosy Posy? We'll all jab at you, you know, and then you must groan like sixty, and tumble all in a heap right here."

"Ess," said the baby, eagerly; "me knows how. Me die booful."

"Yes, Rosy Posy is an awful good dier," said Kitty. "She tumbles ker-flop and just lies still."

This was high praise, for with the Maynards' games of shooting Indians, wild beasts, or captured victims, it was often difficult for the martyred one to lie still without laughing.

"What'll we use for daggers?" said Kitty.

"Here are two ivory paper-knives," said King. "They can't hurt the baby. I don't see any other, except this steel one, and that's most too sharp."

"I'll take that one," said Kitty. "You and Mopsy are so crazy, you might really jab her with it, but I won't."

This was true enough. King and Marjorie were too impetuous in their fun to be trusted with the sharp-pointed paper-knife, but gentle little Kitty never lost her head, and would carefully guard Rosy Posy from any real harm, while seemingly as cruel and belligerent as the others.

"All right, then, here goes!" cried King. "Now, you march to the umbrella-stand and stand there, Baby."

Rosamond obediently toddled on her way, dragging her white draperies, and taking her place as indicated, by the umbrella-stand.

King made the first charge, and, ignoring the text, he lunged at the luckless Cæsar with his ivory dagger, while he gave voice to dire maledictions.

Rosy Posy fell, though the weapon hadn't touched her, and then Marjorie came on to add her make-believe stabs to the wounds already given to the valiant Cæsar. That martyred Roman lay with her eyes closed, ably representing a stabbed Emperor, and Midget poked at her with the paper knife, without causing even a giggle on the part of the very youthful actress.

"Now, Kit—Brutus, I mean—it's your turn. Keep still, Baby, till Kitty stabs you."

"Ess," said Rosy Posy, snuggling into the sofa pillows, and awaiting her final dispatchment.

"Wait a minute," said Kitty, who was poring over the book; "it says, 'Doth not Brutus bootless kneel?' I must take off my shoes."

Kitty was nothing if not literal, so hastily unbuttoning her boots, she flung them off, and a truly bootless Brutus knelt to add more stabs to the defunct Cæsar. The sight of Kitty's black-stockinged feet sticking out from beneath the white draperies, as she knelt, was too much for King, and silently moving toward her, he tickled the soles so temptingly exposed. Kitty, though soulfully declaiming,

"Fly not; stand still; ambition's debt is paid!"

was carefully guarding the point of her steel dagger from Rosy Posy's fat body, but when King tickled her feet, she gave an involuntary kick and fell forward. The sharp steel plunged into the baby's forearm, and was followed by a spurt of blood and a piercing shriek from the child. Kitty, at sight of the blood, gave a short groan and fainted dead away.

King sprang to pick up Rosy Posy, fairly rolling Kitty away to do so, while Marjorie, with a scared, white face, screamed for Nannie, the nurse.

In a moment every one in the house had rushed to them.

Nannie took the shrieking child from King's arms, while Miss Larkin and Marjorie bent over the unconscious Kitty.

Everything was bustle and confusion, but as Sarah brought warm water and a sponge, and Nannie washed the little wounded arm, they found it was only a deep, jagged scratch—bad enough, to be sure—but not a dangerous hurt.

King had already telephoned for the doctor, and in the meantime they all tried to restore Kitty to consciousness.

"She's dead, I'm sure," wailed Miss Larkin, wringing her hands, as she looked at the still little figure lying on the floor. They had put a pillow beneath her head, but Nannie advised them not to move her.

"Oh, no, Miss Larkin; don't say that," pleaded Marjorie; "I'm sure her eye-winkers are fluttering. Wake up, wake up, Kitty dear; Baby's all right. Please wake up."

But Kitty made no response, and Marjorie turned to throw her arms round King's neck, who stood by, looking the picture of hopeless woe.

CHAPTER V
REMORSEFUL ROMANS
"I did it," groaned King; "it was all my fault. Kitty was so careful with that sharp dagger, and then I tickled her feet, and it made her wiggle, and she upset right on the baby. Oh, I've killed dear little Kitty!"

"Maybe you haven't," said Marjorie, hopefully. "Maybe she'll wake up in a minute. And it wasn't your fault anyway, King. You didn't mean to upset her, and anybody's got a right to tickle people's feet."

"No; I ought to have remembered that she had that sharp paper-cutter, and that she might tumble over. It's all my fault."

"It isn't your fault," repeated Marjorie, stoutly. "If it's anybody's fault, it's old Brutus's, for insisting on taking off his boots before he stabbed Cæsar."

Marjorie was sobbing all the while she was talking, and as she stammered out these remarks between her choking sobs, Miss Larkin was not a little perplexed to understand her.

"Brutus? Cæsar? what do you mean?" she asked.

"Oh, we were playing Shakespeare," began Marjorie, "and now I come to think of it, it was all my fault for getting up the game."

Just then, Doctor Mendel arrived, and came briskly into the living-room.

"Well, well!" he exclaimed, in his hearty way; "what's the matter now? Have you young barbarians been breaking each other's bones?"

Then, as he saw Kitty, white and still, upon the floor, he stooped down silently, and bent over the little girl.

"Don't be alarmed," he said, as, after a moment, he looked up and saw the scared and anxious faces watching him; "she'll be all right, soon; have you any smelling salts?"

Marjorie's thoughts flew uncertainly toward the saltcellars in the dining-room, but Miss Larkin answered, "Yes, I have," and running up to her own room, she returned with a vial of Crown Salts.

"That's the ticket!" said the doctor, and carefully holding the dark-green bottle beneath Kitty's nose, he watched her face closely, for he was more afraid of the after-consequences than of her present state.

And, sure enough, as the closed lids fluttered open, and the color came slowly back to the white cheeks, Kitty gave a convulsive shudder, caught sight of Rosy Posy's bandaged arm, and fell into a hysterical crying-fit.

"Take the baby out of the room," commanded the doctor; "and now, Kitty, girl, listen to me. Your little sister is not seriously hurt, but I want to go to her and properly bandage her arm. I can't leave you until you stop this crying—or, at least, partly stop it. So, as long as you keep it up, you are keeping me away from little Rosamond who needs me more than you do."

This was severe talk, but it had the effect, as the doctor intended, of bracing Kitty up to the emergency.

Doctor Mendel knew the little Maynards pretty well. He had attended them through all their childish illnesses, and he knew Kitty's practical, common-sense nature. Had it been Marjorie he was dealing with, he would have chosen another line of argument.

"All right, Doctor," said Kitty, still shaking nervously, but trying hard to stop. "And, anyway, you go to Rosy; there are enough people here to take care of me."

And indeed there seemed to be. Nannie and Sarah had gone off with the baby, but King, Marjorie, and Miss Larkin surrounded the sobbing Kitty, while Ellen and Thomas looked in from the hall doorway, and even James, the coachman, hovered in the background. Kitty's wan smile as she spoke, brought cheer to the watchers, and Doctor Mendel said quietly: "All right, Kitty. I'll take you at your word. I'll go and attend to Rosamond, if you'll promise to try your best not to cry any more. If I hear you screaming again, I shall come right back to you, and that would be the worst harm you could do to Rosy Posy."

"I promise, Doctor," said Kitty, so solemnly that the good old man felt a suspicion of moisture in his own eyes, and Miss Larkin sat bolt up-right, with big tears falling into her brown silk lap.

Doctor Mendel went to the nursery, and unwrapping the little arm that Nurse Nannie had bandaged, carefully examined the wound, which, though only a jagged cut, was a deep one, and had narrowly escaped being a serious affair.

It was necessary to cleanse it thoroughly, and this process was accompanied by piercing shrieks from the suffering child.

These, of course, were unavoidable, for five-year-old Rosy Posy could not be reasoned with like ten-year-old Kitty. So the doctor had to let the child scream, while Nannie held the tiny arm firm for his ministrations. Sarah tried to divert the baby with picture-books and dolls, but all in vain; the heart-rending cries could be heard all over the house.

And here is where Kitty's fine, sensible nature showed itself strongly.

As she heard Rosy Posy's shrieks of pain, it very nearly made her scream in sympathy. But she bravely put her fingers in her ears, and said, with a most pathetic look:

"Don't let me hear her, Mopsy. If I do, I'll cry, and then the doctor will leave her and come down here, and then she'll die—oh, Marjorie!"

Kitty buried her head in her sister's lap, and Marjorie, silently crying herself, held her hands helpfully over Kitty's ears.

Miss Larkin fluttered around like a bewildered hen. She knew she was at the Maynard house for the purpose of taking care of the children in their parents' absence, and here was an emergency—the very first one—and she hadn't the slightest idea of how she could possibly make herself helpful in any way. The doctor and the servants were doing all that could be done for the baby, and Marjorie was comforting Kitty, which was all that could be done for that little girl. Then Miss Larkin's eye fell on Kingdon, who, with hands in his pockets, stood looking out of the window. He was evidently trying hard not to cry, and apparently he, like Miss Larkin, could think of no way to be of any help. Rising, she made her way softly to the boy, and, putting her hand on his shoulder, said:

"Doctor Mendel's fine, isn't he? He'll soon have the baby all right, I'm sure. Suppose you and I pick up those sheets, and put the room to rights a little; Sarah is busy in the nursery."

How often occupation is a help in time of trouble!

Giving Miss Larkin a grateful glance, King turned to look at the room.

The sheets which had waved so gaily as Roman togas, now lay in dejected-looking heaps, the little one, alas! stained by the accident to the baby Cæsar.

Miss Larkin hastily picked up that one, and soon she and King had all the Roman toggery picked up and carried away. They put the furniture back in place, restored "Pompey's Pillar" to its accustomed use as an umbrella-holder, and put all the daggers away in a desk drawer, that they might not unnerve anybody by their sad reminders.

Marjorie, with her loving little ways, had succeeded in quieting Kitty, and as the baby's cries could no longer be heard, things began to look brighter all round.

"Well, well, this is something like!" declared Doctor Mendel, as he returned from the nursery. "You're a trump, Kitty. I know how hard it was for you to brace up to the occasion, but you did it, and you deserve great credit. Now, listen to me, my girl. In the first place, Rosamond is all right. I shall come to see her every day for awhile, to make sure that she keeps all right, but the hurt to her arm is simply a flesh wound, and will heal with only a very slight scar, if any."

"Oh, Doctor!" cried Kitty, shuddering, "will her arm be scarred?"

"Probably not. She is so young, it will doubtless heal without a trace. But even should there be a tiny white mark it will amount to nothing. And, children, listen to this. I attach no blame either to King or Kitty. For children always have tickled each other's toes, and probably always will. The whole affair was an accident, of course. But—I blame all three of you, individually and collectively, for playing with that sharp dagger."

"But Kit is always so careful," broke in Marjorie.

"I know it, and what good did it do? Carefulness cannot always guard against accidents. So promise me that you will never again play any game that includes the use of any dangerous instrument: dagger, knife, scissors, chisel, anything, in fact, that might do physical harm in case of accident."

"Of course we promise," said Marjorie, tearfully. "And we don't have to promise. For we couldn't play with such things after to-day. But, Doctor Mendel, it was all my fault, 'cause I got up the whole game."

"Don't say another word about whose fault it was," interrupted the blunt doctor. "You all agree, I suppose, that it wasn't Rosamond's fault?"

Three astonished and indignant glances answered this question.

"Well, then, I hold that you three older children are equally to blame for playing with what is really a dangerous weapon. Each of you is old enough to know that you ought not to have done so—therefore you are all blameworthy to exactly the same degree. Am I clear?"

"Yes, indeed," said Kitty, sighing. "It seems as if I was the worst. But if you put it that way, I s'pose we all ought to have known better."

27

"Of course we ought," said King. "And I'll never tickle the soles of Kit's feet again, dagger or no dagger."

"I'm glad of that!" said Kitty, fervently, "for, oh, King, I do hate it!"

"All right, old girl. You can play bootless Brutus whenever you like, and I won't tickle you a speck. But your black feet looked so funny coming out from under your white togga."

"White what?" said Doctor Mendel, curiously.

"Her togga. We were all being Romans, you know."

"Oh, I see. Well, you must pronounce that with a long o, my boy; it's toga."

"All right, sir; toga, then. But I don't believe we'll ever play 'Julius Cæsar' again."

"Not with Rosy Posy, anyhow," said Kitty, decidedly.

"But she made a lovely Cæsar," said Midget, reminiscently.

"She must have!" said the doctor, chuckling. "A five-year-old baby girl seems just right for the part!"

Even Kitty laughed at this.

"Well," she said, "she may not have looked just as Cæsar really did, but she looked awful cunning and sweet."

"Here she is!" cried King, and Nurse Nannie came in with the smiling baby in her arms.

In a clean frock, and her lovely hair freshly tied up with a blue ribbon, the little one was quite her usual self. Only the pathetic-looking bandage around the tiny bare arm gave any evidence of the late disaster.

Doctor Mendel carefully watched Kitty as her eyes fell on the bandage. She turned a fiery red, and then went perfectly pale. She choked a little, but by a determined effort of will, she held on to herself, and controlled her agitation.

"Brave little girl!" said Doctor Mendel, patting her shoulder. "You're doing nobly, Kitty, and I have no fears for you now. Remember, if you want to help the baby bear her misfortune, you must do it by unselfishly being bright and cheery, and helping to amuse her, and not by sorrowful regrets that can do no one any good."

"Yes, sir," said Kitty, meekly, but with a note of strong determination in her voice. "But I wish Mother was home. Shall I write her about it all, Doctor?"

Doctor Mendel was such an old and tried friend of the Maynard family, that the children consulted him on any subject, with full confidence in his sympathy and wisdom.

"Well, I don't know, Kitty. I hate to have you go all over the matter in a letter, when really it is now a thing of the past. And yet I suppose you wouldn't sleep quietly in your little bed, if you didn't tell Mother about it at once. Well—how's this plan? Suppose I write and tell her about it, and then she'll write to you, and then you can keep it up as long as you choose after that."

"Oh, that will be fine, Doctor!" cried Kitty, her heart full of thankfulness for his kindness. She had dreaded to write the awful story, and yet she wanted her mother to know about it, and this plan was a relief to her burdened little heart.

And Doctor Mendel's fine insight told him all this. He knew that emotional, sensitive little Kitty would live over the scene as she wrote about it, and her remorse and self-censure would work cruelly upon her already overwrought nerves. So he determined to write himself, and tell the story in its true light, knowing that Mr. and Mrs. Maynard pretty thoroughly understood their own children, and would at once appreciate the situation. Then the doctor went away, and without his cheery presence, the children's spirits lagged again.

Then it was that Miss Larkin came to the rescue.

"Now, children," she said, and though her bright gaiety of manner always seemed a little forced and unreal, they listened politely to what she was about to say.

"Now, dear children," she repeated, "after a dreadful scene, such as we've just passed through, I don't think there's anything so cheering and comforting as an extra good dinner."

"Hooray!" cried King, who had expected a lecture or, at best, a talk of a consolatory nature; "I say, Larky, you're a brick!"

He stopped, suddenly overcome with discomfiture at having all unintentionally used the nickname that he had promised never to say again.

But, to his great surprise, Miss Larkin laughed gaily. "Good for you, King!" she said; "I used to have a chum who called me 'Larky,' but I haven't heard the name for years. I'd like it if you'd use it often."

"But—but," stammered King, "I promised Mother I wouldn't. She said it was disrespectful."

Miss Larkin laughed again. "So it would be if you meant it disrespectfully. But if you and I can be chums, and I ask you to use it, then I know Mother would have no objections."

"I know it, too," said Marjorie; "can't we all be chums—Larky?"

She said the name so sweetly, and after a momentary hesitation, that Miss Larkin promptly kissed her.

"Yes," she declared. "We'll all be chums together, and you shall all call me Larky, and I'll call you by your nicknames. Now, for this cheering dinner of ours. It is belated anyway, but I think by a judicious use of the telephone we can add enough to it to make it a special feast. Kitty, what would you like better than anything else?"

"Ice cream," said Kitty, so promptly, that one would almost think she had been expecting the question.

"You'll get it," said Miss Larkin, with a decided wag of her head. "Now, Mopsy, what will you choose?"

"Little iced cakes," said Marjorie; "green ones, and yellow ones, and pink and white and choclit ones."

"King next," went on the questioner. "Of course, you must choose something that can be bought, not made."

"Nuts and raisins," said King, after a moment's thought.

Then Rosy Posy announced her desire for "fig-crackers," and the menu was made up.

Miss Larkin bustled away to the telephone, and after a colloquy with the caterer, arranged to have the order sent up at once.

As the dainties desired were all of the nature of dessert, there was no need to delay dinner, and when Sarah announced it, the children realized that they were decidedly hungrier than usual—which was saying a great deal!

By virtue of her position as heroine of the day, Rosy Posy was allowed to sit up to dinner, and though she fell asleep at the table, with a "fig-cracker" in her hand, she was carried away to bed without interrupting the festivities.

And festivities they were. For a sort of reaction from the late tragic events, and the fact that ice cream always made a "party," so enlivened their drooping spirits that the little Maynards were their own gay selves once more, and "Larky" proved that upon occasion she could be as merry as her nickname sounded.

CHAPTER VI
LETTERS AND CARDS

"It's awful to have Father and Mother away so long, but it's lovely to get their letters," said Marjorie, as Sarah brought in a big budget of mail that the postman had just brought. The Maynards were at breakfast, and as King distributed the various letters, postcards, and parcels, there proved to be something for everybody at the table.

Mr. and Mrs. Maynard were now in Florida, and they sent many souvenirs of their trip.

Marjorie had a silver teaspoon, King a book-mark, Kitty a pin-tray, and Rosy Posy a queer little doll, all of which were marked with the name of the beautiful hotel where the travellers were then staying.

Miss Larkin received a lovely lace handkerchief, which was a more elaborate gift than the others, though not so specially a souvenir.

Then each had two or three postcards of the Florida scenery, and, best of all, each had a letter addressed separately and individually.

As they eagerly opened and read them, Rosy Posy, only slightly assisted by Sarah, also opened her letter and pretended to read it, nodding her curly head and smiling as if she could really make out the written pages.

And then, each in turn, they read their letters aloud.

"Is yours in poetry, Miss Larkin?" asked Marjorie. "Ours are."

"Partly," said Miss Larkin, smiling. "Your father is quite a poet, isn't he?"

"He says he isn't," said Kitty; "but I think his verses are lovely. You read yours out first, Miss Larkin, and then we'll read ours."

So Miss Larkin began:

"Dear Miss Larkin, here we are

Seeming near, though really far.

Wondering how you get along

With those children, so headstrong.

Are your dark locks turning gray

With their worry day by day?

Are they jumping at the chance

To be leading you a dance?

Or has your devoted care

Tamed them into angels fair?

Well, whate'er may be the case,

We are glad you're in our place.

So forgive their naughty pranks,

And accept our love and thanks—

Blessings be upon your head:

Always yours,

Helen and Ed."

"Oh, isn't that lovely!" sighed Kitty. "I 'spect they made that up together. They can both make rhymes, you know."

"You next, King," said Marjorie. "We always go by ages, you know."

"All right," said King. "Mine isn't very long. I guess Father wrote it all himself.

31

"Dear old King,

Everything

Is going fine,

So here's a line

To let you know

That, as we go,

Our thoughts turn back

Along the track

Until, in our mind's eye, we see

Our King Cole and his Sisters Three.

So to the girls and to the brother

We send much love,

Father and Mother."

"That's a nice one," said Kitty, who loved the jingles. "Now I'll read mine. Oh, no, it's your turn first, Mops."

"Mine's from Mother. I guess she thinks I'm up to some mischief. She says:

"Marjorie, dear, dearie, derious,

I think I'll write you a line that's serious—

Only to say, Be good, sweet child,

And don't do anything wrong or wild.

If mischievous pranks you want to play,

Put them off till a future day.

For I would rather at home be found

When Marjorie Mischief comes around.

But I feel quite sure I need feel no fears,

For my bonnie lassie of twelve sweet years

Is trying, I know, to be good as gold.

So here's all the love that a heart can hold

To my darling Daughter, far away

From your ownest, lovingest

Mothery May."

"May is short for Maynard," Marjorie explained to Miss Larkin. "We often call her Mothery May. It's such a pretty name."

"Yes, it is," said Miss Larkin. "I didn't know Helen could rhyme as well as that."

"She learned it from Father," said Kitty. "She told me so once. She says it isn't poetry, it's just jingle. But I love it all. We're going to save all these letters and cards and things, and make a big scrap-book."

"That will be fine," said Miss Larkin. "Let's begin it at once. I'll help you."

"All right; thank you," said Kitty. "Now I'll read mine.

"Kitty, Kitty, Kitty,

What an awful pity

That we couldn't have you here

To enjoy this country, dear.

You would love the sky and sun

And the blossoms, every one.

And the waves upon the shore,

Rolling, tumbling, o'er and o'er.

Never mind, Miss Kittiwinks,

Sometime it will chance, methinks,

That we'll come down here again

And we'll bring you with us then.

You and King and Mops, and maybe

That small Rosy Posy baby!

Now, good-bye, for I've no time

To waste on further foolish rhyme.

I don't like to work my brain hard.

From your fond old

Father Maynard."

"Oh," cried Kitty, "don't you just love that! Brain hard and Maynard is a grand rhyme!"

"Great!" agreed King, "though it joggles a little, I think."

"Well, of course, it isn't a real rhyme," said Kitty, looking thoughtful; "it's just a sort of a joke rhyme. That's why I like it so much. Now, Rosy Posy, I'll read yours."

"Ess, Kitty; wead it out loud to me."

"I want my Rosy Posy,

  Yes, I do!

I want to cuddle cosy

  Just with you.

I want my little girlie,

  Pink and white;

Hair so soft and curly,

  Eyes so bright.

There are but a few, love,

  Sweet as you.

Rosy Posy, Truelove,

  I love you."

"Oh," exclaimed Kitty, enraptured, "what a sweet little love-poem! Why, it's a valentine!"

"Ess," said the happy recipient; "it's my ballytine. Muvver sended it all to me."

"So she did, Baby," said Midget. "And it's a lovely one. We'll put it in the big scrap-book. Now, Miss Larkin, I must skip to school."

"So say we all of us," said King, rising from the table. "Let's put all these letters and gifts and things away together, and get them out again to-night. Can we begin the scrap-book to-night, Miss Larkin?"

"Yes, King, I'll get the book to-day. I'd like to make you a present of it."

"Oh, thank you, Miss Larkin. You're a trump! You'll sure get it, won't you?"

"Yes, indeed. I have to go downtown this afternoon, and I'll get a real nice one."

"Mayn't I take all the postcards over to Delight's with me?" said Marjorie. "I want to show them to her and to Miss Hart."

"Sure, take mine," said King, heartily; and Kitty, too, was willing.

"I'll be awful careful of 'em," said Midget. "And I know Miss Hart will be so interested to see them."

Miss Hart was, indeed, interested. She changed her mind about the lessons she had planned for the day, and took Florida for the theme instead. She had been there herself, so she recognized the places pictured on the postcards, and described them in a most interesting way. The map of Florida was found in the Geography, and Miss Hart told her pupils all about its wonderful fruits and flowers. Then, taking down a United States History, she read to them of the settlement of the state, of its growth and present condition, and many other interesting details. The other Southern states were touched on, and when the lesson was over Delight and Marjorie felt quite well informed about that section of our country.

Then Miss Hart asked them each to write a short composition about Florida. These she corrected, and explained her corrections so clearly that, almost without knowing it, the girls had had a lesson in English composition.

"Oh," sighed Marjorie, as she put on her hat to go home; "it has been a lovely morning. Isn't it strange, Miss Hart, how I used to hate to go to school, and now I just love it."

Miss Hart smiled.

"You hate routine work, Marjorie," she said; "and you disliked the confinement and discipline of the regular schoolroom. Our lessons are so varied and unsystematic, they don't tire you in the same way."

"They don't tire me at all, Miss Hart; but it is you who make them so pleasant. Nobody else ever could teach things as you do. You make lessons seem play."

"They are play, if you enjoy them. Anything we enjoy is a recreation, and, therefore, pleasant."

"You're coming over this afternoon, you know, Mops; the Jinks Club meets here."

"'Course I am, Delight. We're all coming. What are we going to do?"

"I don't know. Miss Hart said she'd help us. You know, my mother won't let us rampage all over the house, as your mother does."

"I know it," said Marjorie, smiling to think of Mrs. Spencer's carefully placed furniture and immaculately kept rooms, subjected to such invasions as frequently turned the Maynard house topsy-turvy.

"In fact," Delight went on, "Mother says I can't have the Jinks Club meet here, unless we promise to stay in just the two rooms—the library and dining-room."

"All right," assented Midget, cheerfully. "We can have plenty of fun in two rooms. Can't we, Miss Hart?"

"Yes, I'm sure you can. Quiet fun, you know. And perhaps you'll enjoy that—for a change, you know."

"I know we'll enjoy it, if you're with us, Miss Hart," and with a loving good-bye to the governess and to Delight, Midget scampered home.

"Oh, fiddlesticks!" said King, as, at the luncheon table, Marjorie told of the meeting of the Club that afternoon. "I don't see any fun cooped up in two rooms. Why can't we play outdoors?"

"Oh, Mrs. Spencer hardly ever lets Delight go out to play in March. She says it's a dangerous month."

"Huh! We play outdoors any day in the year."

"I know we do, King. 'Cause Mother wants us to. But Mrs. Spencer is different."

"Different! I should say she was! She's about as much like our mother as chalk's like cheese. Let's have the Club over here, Mops."

"No," said Marjorie, looking thoughtful. "I think we'd better not have it here while Mother's away. For you know we always break things, or 'most kill ourselves, and after 'Julius Cæsar' I think we want to beware of our sort of games."

"My! but you're getting cautious! Well, all right; I'll go to Delight's this time, but if it's poky, I won't go again. Anyway, it'll be at Flip Henderson's next time, and I guess we'll have fun there."

"I'd just as lieve play quiet games, anyway," put in Kitty. "I've had enough of accidents."

She glanced at Rosy Posy's bandaged arm, which, though it didn't incommode the baby in the least, was a silent reminder to the others.

So, at three o'clock, the three Maynards went across the street to Delight's house.

Dorothy Adams and Flip Henderson came at the same time, and they all went in together.

It is strange how the atmosphere of a home will affect its guests.

Mrs. Spencer was a kind and pleasant lady enough, and yet no sooner were the members of the Jinks Club inside her house, than they suddenly became silent and a little self-conscious. They had an undefined feeling that they must "behave," and it made them a little stiff and unnatural.

The Maynard house, on the other hand, was like a playground. Once inside those hospitable doors, they felt an unspoken welcome that was homelike and cordial to the last degree.

So they decorously laid off their hats and coats, taking pains to place them neatly on the hatrack or hall table, and then primly seated themselves around the library. King began to fidget; he was always impatient under restraint of any sort. But Marjorie felt more at home in the Spencer house, and, too, she had faith in Miss Hart's plans, whatever they might be.

Kitty was of an adaptable nature, and didn't care much what they played. Dorothy was with her, and that was fun of itself.

Soon Miss Hart came in, and her smiling face, and cordial manner, did much to cheer the hearts of the Jinks Club.

"I was so interested in Marjorie's postcards," she began, "that I thought you might like to play a postcard game this afternoon. So I've arranged it for you. As you see, in this room, and the dining-room, are many postcards pinned to the walls and window-frames, and on tables and mantels. Some are partly hidden, others in plain sight. In every case the printed title is cut off, and each card is numbered. Now, we will go travelling."

This began to look promising. King glanced around at the postcards, and noticed some attractive-looking parcels tied with ribbons, and decided it was to be a sort of a party. Now, a party was about as much fun as a regular Jinks Club meeting, so his spirits rose to the occasion.

"Here is your luggage," Miss Hart went on, giving each a pencil and blank card. "Write down the number of any postcard, and write against it what you think it represents. Don't look at each other's lists, and the one who has most correct answers will receive a prize. Good-bye, my tourist friends; start now on your travels."

It was fun. Some of the pictures were impossible to mistake. The Eiffel Tower, the Pyramids of Egypt, and the Bunker Hill Monument were easily recognized. But others were not so well known, and sometimes the tourists had to think hard to remember where some of the buildings or monuments were situated. The scenes were from all over the world; from the Coliseum in Rome to the Flatiron Building in New York; and the Jinks members giggled when they came across a picture of their own town library and the Rockwell Railway Station. It was an absorbing game, and the tourists went about from picture to picture, and then back on their tracks again to try once more to recall some half-forgotten arch or statue.

At last, the allotted time was up, and the tourists all returned to the library, while Miss Hart looked over the cards. To her surprise, King had the greatest number of correct answers, for though he was the oldest one present, he had not studied ancient history as much as Marjorie and Delight had.

"How do you happen to be so well-informed?" asked Miss Hart, as she handed him the first prize.

"I don't know," said King. "I think I see pictures in the illustrated papers, and somehow I remember them."

"That's what we call a 'photographic memory,'" said Miss Hart, smiling, "and it's a very good thing to have."

CHAPTER VII
A JINKS PARTY

The second prize was really won by Delight, but as she was hostess, of course she wouldn't take it, so, Flip Henderson having the next best list, the prize was given to him.

"Well," remarked Midget, "that's a pretty thing! Only two boys in our Jinks Club, and they take the two prizes!"

"You girls will have to look to your laurels," said Miss Hart, laughingly.

As the prizes were both postcard albums, they were equally appropriate for a boy or girl, and the two boys who won them were secretly quite proud of their achievement.

"Now, we've time for one more game," said Miss Hart, "and this is one without prizes, but I think you'll say it's good fun. Kitty and Dorothy, will you distribute these bits of paper, keeping them blank side up?"

The two little girls took the box of small papers, and gave them out to the others, being careful not to look at the written side. The slips were about an inch long, and half an inch wide, and though the girls tried honestly not to look, they couldn't help seeing there was a single word written on each one.

At last, all were distributed, and the children sat round the room waiting for the game to begin.

"This is a lovely Jinks Club meeting," said Dorothy Adams. "I like it better than the ones where we romp so hard."

"It's sure lots of fun," agreed King. "But it's just like a party. Jinks Club never was like a party before."

"I don't care what it's like, if you all have a good time," said Delight, who had been afraid the "Jinksies" wouldn't have a good time at her house, where romping was not allowed.

"We're having a beautiful time," Marjorie said, as she squeezed Delight's arm.

Then Miss Hart began the game.

"I will tell a story," she said, "and when I pause, King, who sits next to me, will turn over one of his papers and read the word on it. Then I'll go on, and when I pause again, Dorothy, who sits next, will turn over one of her papers and read it out. And so on, round the circle. Each one of you be ready in turn, please, so as not to delay the thrilling tale. Now we'll start. Once upon a time a gentleman was walking down a crowded city street, when he suddenly saw a———"

"Giraffe," said King, who had his paper all ready to read.

" 'What a strange thing!' exclaimed the gentleman. 'But I will lead it away from here lest it scare somebody.' So he persuaded the giraffe to go with him, and, stopping at a shop, he bought a———"

"Sunbonnet," said Dorothy.

The children all laughed, but Miss Hart went on:

" 'Just the thing!' exclaimed the man. 'Without this, my poor giraffe might have been sun-struck.' He tied the sunbonnet on the giraffe's head, although, to do so, he had to climb up on a——"

"Bureau," said Midget.

"Which was just about to be placed on a moving-van. The sunbonnet properly adjusted, the gentleman said politely to the giraffe, 'What is your name?' To his surprise, the animal spoke quite plainly, and answered——"

"Strawberry Jam," read Delight, giggling.

" 'A lovely name!' exclaimed the man. 'Now, Strawberry Jam, I feel sure you are hungry, so I will feed you some——' "

"Tin tacks," said Kitty.

" 'You may not think you'll like them, dear Strawberry Jam, but I assure you that, made up into little cakes, and iced over with——' "

"Mucilage!"

" 'They are really very nice.' 'Not for me!' growled the giraffe. 'I much prefer——' "

"Soap and candles."

" 'Very well,' exclaimed the man, 'you shall have those also. Now, as you're weary, I propose you take a nap in a——' "

"Washboiler!"

"It was difficult to get the large animal in, but by doubling him up the gentleman managed to get Strawberry Jam quite comfortably in the washboiler, when just then a lady came along. She carried——"

"Two watermelons."

"And——"

"A live turkey."

"And——"

"A pail of whitewash."

"Setting down her burdens, she said to the man, 'I belong to the Society for the Prevention of——' "

"Green apples."

" 'And I shall have you arrested for ill-treating that giraffe, unless you at once give him a——
——' "

"Lace collar."

" 'I shall carry out my threat.'

" 'Madame,' said the gentleman, 'I have no lace collars handy, and, besides, with his long neck, he would require about seventeen, but I will give him a——' "

"Yellow wheelbarrow."

" 'Do so!' cried the lady, 'and I will wheel him away in it.' She did so, and the giraffe was never seen or heard of again."

"Oh, Miss Hart, don't stop! We have several papers left yet!" cried Kitty, as the story came to an abrupt end.

"I must, dearie, for I see Mary is ready to announce supper."

"Supper!" exclaimed Midget. "Why, we never have supper at Jinks Club! Just cookies and lemonade or plain water."

"But this is to make up for your being so good and quiet," said Mrs. Spencer, who stood in the doorway leading to the dining-room. "I've been told that Jinks Club usually necessitates a whole redecoration of the house, but I can't see that you've done the least bit of damage here today. So here's your reward."

It was a very inviting-looking reward, for the dining-table was set prettily, and with Mrs. Spencer and Miss Hart at either end, the six children were soon seated in their places.

No crackers and lemonade this time! There were creamed oysters, and little sandwiches, and cocoa, and afterward a lovely snow pudding and tiny iced cakes and bonbons.

The feast was delicious, but somehow conversation seemed to flag.

Mrs. Spencer was charmingly hospitable, but she was so polite, that it made the children feel restrained.

"Do you miss your mother, Marjorie?" asked the hostess, in her conversational way, and Midget answered:

"Yes, Mrs. Spencer, very much."

It sounded too short, but poor Midge couldn't think of anything to add to the bald statement.

King helped her out. The Maynards always tried to help each other.

40

"We all miss Mother," he said, "and Father, too."

"But we try to be cheerful about it," supplemented Kitty, who had an uncomfortable feeling that she must act as if at a "party."

Then a silence fell, and had it not been for Miss Hart's cheery little jokes and merry manner, the supper would have been a very quiet affair.

At half-past five they all went home, and, after polite good-byes, the three Maynards walked decorously across the street.

But as they entered their own gate, King cried out:

"Race you to the house!" and the three broke into a mad run for dear life.

Of course, King got there first, but plump Marjorie, puffing and blowing, came a close second, while Kitty, usually a swift runner, came walking behind them with great dignity.

"I can't get off my Spencery air so soon," she explained, and the others laughed, for Kitty was far more inclined toward elegant repose of manner than the other two madcaps.

"Huh! Guess you'll have to!" cried King, and, taking her two hands in his own with a clinching grip, he began to whirl her round and round. This somewhat dangerous game, known as "Sail a boat," required careful attention, if accidents were to be avoided; so, seeing she was in for it, Kitty gracefully capitulated and swung round faster and faster until she nearly had King off his feet.

"There, stop it!" commanded Marjorie. "You'll get dizzy, and then you're sure to fall. Quit it, King! We don't want any more accidents!"

"That's so," agreed King, stopping slowly, and helping Kitty to preserve her equilibrium.

"But I do say," he went on, as they all three burst in at the front door together, "I'd rather have plain, everyday Jinks than to go to a Spencer party."

"Oh, I don't know," said Marjorie, who was always satisfied with things as they came. "I liked the party part of it, and the supper was grand."

"But it was so mixed up," said Kitty. "In the first place, it wasn't a party, 'cause there was no ice cream, and yet it was a party, 'cause we sat at the table, and had the cut-glass goblets. Then, it wasn't a party, 'cause we weren't dressed up, and yet it was a party, 'cause the grown-ups helped entertain us."

"That's the point, Kit," said her brother. "It wasn't either party or Jinks Club, but a mixture of both. I'd rather have either one thing or the other. But I'll make up for it now. I was so 'fraid I'd cut up jinks over there, I didn't know what to do. But here goes!"

Like one let suddenly loose from restraint, King turned two or three handsprings down the long hall, and at the last one managed to collide with both Miss Larkin and Rosamond's doll-carriage. The three were pretty well tangled up; King lost his balance, Miss Larkin lost her dignity, and the doll-carriage lost a wheel.

41

But King was in high spirits by this time.

"There, there, Larky," he said, "you're all right. Pick up her back comb, Mops. Don't step on her eyeglasses, Kitty! Look out, they're right under your feet!"

Fortunately the comb and glasses were rescued intact and restored to their owner.

Miss Larkin didn't quite know whether to be annoyed or to laugh, but King was in a wheedlesome mood, and he patted her shoulders, and smoothed down her laces as he said:

"There, Larky Parky; it's all right. You're not mussed up a bit. Nothing's busted but the carriage. And I guess we can get that wheel fixed. And, Jiminetty Christmas! I had to tumble about a little, to get limbered up after that stiff party. Oh, I say, Larky, dear, did you get us our scrap-book, as you promised?"

"Oh, I didn't!" exclaimed Miss Larkin, looking greatly chagrined. "To tell you the truth, King, I forgot all about it."

"It's naughty to be forgetful."

"Yes, King, I know it is; and I'm awfully sorry. But I had a letter from some friends who are coming to visit me here, and everything else went out of my mind."

The Maynard children had already had some experience with Miss Larkin's forgetfulness, so they were not greatly surprised.

But they were disappointed, and Kitty's face showed it so plainly, that Miss Larkin said:

"I'll do my best to repair my error, Kitty. I'll go downtown to-night, right after dinner, and get the scrap-book."

"Oh, no, Miss Larkin, you needn't do that," said Marjorie, quite overcome by this offer. "It's too late and too dark for you to go out alone. Unless," she added, as an afterthought, "we all go with you."

"Oh, let us do that," begged Kitty. "I've almost never been downtown at night. Oh, do let's go! It would be lovely!"

"Would that make up to you for my forgetfulness?" asked Miss Larkin, smiling, and when they all chorused, "Yes!" she agreed to take them.

Dinner was soon over, for after their Jinks supper, the children wanted almost nothing, and then, scrambling into their coats and hats, they declared themselves ready.

Kitty walked with Miss Larkin, and King and Midget followed.

"Oh!" sighed Kitty, as they came at last to the brightly-lighted Main Street, "isn't it wonderful. They say New York is very brilliant at night, but I don't think it can be much brighter than this. Is it, Miss Larkin?"

"Oh, yes, indeed it is, Kitty. Have you never seen New York at night?"

"No; Mother says I'm too young. I'm not ten yet, you know. But I don't see how it can be much gayer than this."

The Main Street of Rockwell was the usual thoroughfare of a small town, but the bright electrics in many of the shop-windows gave it a fairly light effect.

One large drug-shop, which, of course, was open evenings, kept stationery, and here they went for the scrap-book.

Great care was exercised in choosing it, for if too small, it would not hold enough, and the very large ones were unwieldy.

So just the right size was selected, and King volunteered to carry it home.

Miss Larkin was warmly thanked by her appreciative beneficiaries, and then, as they turned toward home, she said:

"Suppose we make this a sort of gala night, and stop here at this shop and have some ice cream."

"Oh!" exclaimed Kitty, ecstatically, "do let's do that!"

The others were far from unwilling, so the quartette were soon seated round a white marble-topped table.

"I do think," said Kitty, as she viewed lovingly the pink and white heap that was placed in front of her, "I do think we're having the loveliest time!"

"Better than the Jinks Club?" asked Miss Larkin, with a twinkle in her eye.

"Well, different," said Kitty. "I feel as if I could talk every-day talk, you know, and not think how it's going to sound."

"I do hate to have to think how things sound," admitted King, honestly.

"But I s'pose," said Midget, thoughtfully, "we ought to talk always so they sound all right anyway."

"That sentence might be improved upon," said Miss Larkin, laughing; "but I want you to have a specially good time this evening, so never mind about any frills on your conversation. I've been thinking, children, that I've rather neglected you. I ought to do more to entertain and amuse you, now that your dear parents are away."

The three Maynards looked at her in amazement. They had thought that Miss Larkin was very indulgent usually; and though sometimes she was unexpectedly strict or stern, yet in a moment she would forget what she had said, and give them an extra treat of some sort. The truth was, Miss Larkin was decidedly inconsistent. All unused to the management of children, she was now over-indulgent and now over-exacting. She had no knowledge of the uniformly mild and gentle, yet positive government which Mr. and Mrs. Maynard exercised in their home.

And so the Maynard children, not understanding this, had accepted Miss Larkin as she was, and though they sometimes rebelled at her really unjust commands, they enjoyed to the full her often unwise indulgence. Now, they were surprised, indeed, to hear her say she had neglected them, but with their easy adaptability they were quite ready to accept present and future favors. However, King felt that justice was due her, so he said:

"Oh, come now, Miss Larkin; you've been pretty good to us. I think you're a brick, don't you, girls?"

"Yes, we do," agreed Midge and Kitty, and then Marjorie went on:

"Did you say you expect company, Miss Larkin? Perhaps we can help you get ready for them."

Miss Larkin smiled, as she remembered the "decorations" that met her eyes the day she arrived at the Maynard house, and she replied:

"No; you can't help me, except by keeping out of the way as much as possible, and behaving as well as you can while they're here."

"We'll try," said Marjorie, earnestly; "who are they, Miss Larkin?"

"Mr. and Mrs. Mortimer, some friends of mine from Boston. They will stay two or three days. And I want to have everything as nice as possible, for they are rather particular people."

"H'm," said King. "If there's anything I don't go much on, it's these 'rather particular people.' But to please you, Miss Larkin, I'll promise to behave the very bestest I can. And if the girls don't do likewise, I'll pound 'em."

"Huh!" said Midget, "guess you'd get pounded back!"

"Oh, children," said Miss Larkin, in despair; "don't talk like that! I know you don't mean anything, for you love each other, but your rough and tumble 'poundings' would shock Mrs. Mortimer inexpressibly."

"All right, Larky, dear," said King, in his winning way; "we won't have any jinks of any kind while your friends are here. We'll be as good—as good—oh, we'll be just Spencer good!"

"That's nice of you," said Miss Larkin, beaming on them; "and if you say so, I know you'll keep your word."

CHAPTER VIII
ROMPS AND RHYMES
For the next few days the children were left to their own devices. Miss Larkin was busy as a bee getting the house ready for her expected company. The two pretty guest rooms were appointed for their use, and Miss Larkin herself moved into Mrs. Maynard's room.

Astonishing preparations were made in the kitchen department, and even Ellen, the good-natured cook, was amazed at the lavish orders given to the grocer, butcher, and caterer.

"Shure, an' annybuddy'd think the hull rile fam'ly was a-comin'," she said to Sarah.

But they were well-trained servants, and as Miss Larkin was temporarily mistress of the house, they obeyed her wishes.

The day that the Mortimers were expected, the children came home from school to find the house in specially immaculate order, flowers in almost every room, and a general air of festivity all about.

"We have only a 'pick-up' luncheon," said Miss Larkin, who was looking over a timetable as she talked. "You see, I forgot to order anything—I was so absorbed in my dinner preparations. But Ellen has found something for you, I see."

And, indeed, Ellen had not forgotten the children's midday appetites, and so there was plenty to eat, if not so carefully served as usual.

"I don't want to hurry you too much," Miss Larkin went on, as they sat down to the table, "but please get through as soon as you can; for I want the table lengthened, and then I shall myself set it for dinner."

"We'll make sandwiches, and take 'em up in the playroom to eat, if you say so, Miss Larkin," volunteered Kingdon, who was willing to help in any way he could.

"Mercy, no, child! That would only make extra work for Sarah, clearing up after you. No, eat your lunch here. Don't gobble, but make all the haste you can."

This was a rather mixed direction, and caused much hilarity among the young Maynards.

"I'll spread my bread on both sides," announced Marjorie, "that'll use up my butter faster."

"I'll put sugar on mine," declared Kitty, quick to see the possibilities of this new game; "so, you see, I can eat butter and sugar both at once, and so hurry up things."

"I'll eat with both hands," giggled King, as he broke a slice of bread in two, and took alternate bites.

"Oh, children!" exclaimed Miss Larkin, in despair, "now you've commenced carrying on, I don't know where you'll end up! I know how you act when you once begin your nonsense!"

"Aw, truly, Larky, we're going to be good," said King, in the wheedling tone that often betokened "cutting up." "And as I know you want this table to set for King and Queen Mortimer, I'll now remove all these bothering children. Girls, I'll race you to the front door!"

Marjorie jumped up, dropping her fork and upsetting a cup of cocoa; Kitty flew after her, over-turning her chair as she ran; but as the girls reached the door between the dining-room and hall, King slammed it to, and turned the key on the other side.

This meant they couldn't reach the front door, except by going through the kitchen and thence to the hall again. Of course, King would get there before them, but this was all the more reason to fly after him and avenge themselves. Back they ran around the table. Midget tripped over the rug, caught at the tablecloth, and upset a glass of water on her head.

Kitty paused to lift Rosy Posy down from her high chair, for the baby was clamoring to join the fray.

Through the pantry and into the kitchen the whirlwind passed, nearly upsetting Ellen and Sarah on their mad flight to the front hall.

Miss Larkin, still at the table, sat looking distracted. What would the Mortimers think of such actions as these! And the Maynard children, even when meaning to behave their best, were so easily started off on a romp by the least provocation.

"Look at that!" said Miss Larkin, as Sarah came in. "A nice mess, just as I'm preparing for a dinner party!"

"Yes'm," said Sarah, respectfully. "But them children do be in such a hurry sometimes. I'll clear it all up, mem. And then I'll help ye with the table."

But Miss Larkin was really irate, and Sarah's air of apology for the children only made her more so.

"Call them to me, Sarah," she said. "I wish to speak to them."

Sarah obediently went in search of the children, and found them in a scrambled heap near the front door. A good-natured wrestling match was on and, as a consequence, hair ribbons and neckties were off.

"She wants you," said Sarah, as she looked at the by no means unfamiliar performance. "I'll take Rosy Posy, and the rest of ye had better go, an' have it over with."

"Come on, then," said King, already sorry for their boisterous misdemeanors.

Unlocking the door, he marched into the dining-room, followed by his two sisters.

"Dear Miss Larkin," he said, with a low and elaborate bow, "we're 'ceedingly sorry we went off in such a hurry, and we've come back to 'pollergize."

Kitty caught the dramatic tone of his apology, and falling on her knees, with clasped hands, she looked beseechingly up into Miss Larkin's face, and wailed:

"Do forgive us—ah, do!"

Marjorie, not to be outdone, fell down in a posture which she fondly hoped represented an Oriental salaam.

Crouching on the floor, she buried her face in her folded arms, and rocked her plump body from side to side, as, she gave voice to long, deep groans supposed to be expressive of abject repentance. Her position was temptingly insecure, and King couldn't resist a tiny push which sent her rolling over against Kitty, and the girls both lost their equilibrium.

Then Miss Larkin lost her temper.

"You're the worst children I ever saw!" she exclaimed. "I didn't know civilized beings could be such rude and unmannerly and barbarous——"

"Cannibals," prompted King, as she paused for lack of a sufficiently opprobrious name.

46

This made the girls giggle, and they at once began to eat each other, in dumb show.

But Miss Larkin saw nothing humorous in the situation.

"I don't see how I can have those people," she went on. "I invited them, thinking you children would at least act fairly decent, and now as you've begun this hoodlum business, I just know you'll keep it up and mortify me to death."

"No, we won't," declared King. "Honest and truly, black and bluely, Miss Larkin, we'll begin now, and we'll be as good as pie—custard pie!"

"Mince pie!" supplemented Marjorie.

"Lemon meringue pie," said Kitty, rolling her eyes, as she thought of a lovely big one even now on the pantry shelf.

"If I could only trust you," said Miss Larkin, sighing. "But I can't. You're too uncertain."

"Oh, no, we aren't," said King, sidling up to her, and patting her shoulder. "And, anyway, after a bang-up tussle, like that, we're always better'n ever, for a long time."

"Yes, we are," corroborated Kitty; "it's what Father calls the clam after the storm. Oh, Miss Larkin, we will be good!"

"You ought to be punished," said the tormented lady, looking at the merry, if repentant, faces.

"Oh, do punish us!" cried Marjorie. "That would square it all up; and, besides, punishments are gen'rally fun. You can most always make a game out of 'em."

"You can, can you!" exclaimed Miss Larkin; "well, I rather think I'll give you a punishment that you can't make a noisy game out of, at any rate. Now, listen to me. I expect my friends on the five o'clock train. I shall go in the carriage to meet them at the station. At half-past four, I want you all to be dressed nicely, and wait in the drawing-room till we return. Marjorie, you may wear your new white serge; and, Kitty, put on your light-blue voile."

"Yes'm," said the two little girls.

"Now, be sure to allow time enough to make your toilets properly, but before that you must each learn a piece of poetry and recite it to me without missing a word. This is your punishment, and I trust it will at least keep you quiet for the afternoon."

It was, indeed, a punishment. The Maynard children loved to read poetry, or have it read to them, but memorizing it was another matter.

"How long a poem, Miss Larkin?" asked Kitty, disconsolately.

Miss Larkin considered. If she set them a long task, they might not get through in time to dress; if a short one, time would be left for mischief.

"About ten lines," she said, at last. "Not less than ten, and more, if you choose."

"May we select our poems ourselves?"

"Yes; that is, you may take anything that you find printed in any book in the library. Now, go on, and when you have learned them, I will hear you recite them."

The three culprits walked slowly away to their punishment, and Miss Larkin felt satisfied that she had at least quelled their boisterous spirits for a time.

She turned to her own occupations, and was soon lost in the pleasant flutter of arranging her elaborate dinner-table.

The three in the library stared at the book-shelves.

"Ten lines!" muttered King. "I'm going to pick out something with short lines, I can tell you."

"I wish she hadn't said 'printed,'" said Marjorie; "then I'd learn some of the poems Mother and Father write us in letters. That would be fun."

"I'll tell you what," said Kitty. "Let's learn things out of our scrap-book. Don't you know, the one Mother made, and pasted in verses cut out of the papers and magazines."

"That's so!" cried King. "They're printed, sure enough; and a lot more fun than these Tennysons and Longfellows sitting up here on the shelves."

Kitty brought the scrap-book, and the three sat down on the floor to look it over. It was a jolly book, filled with pictures and jingles, and they became so interested in reading it, that they almost forgot they were being punished.

"Well, I s'pose we must each pick out one to learn," said King, at last. "I guess I'll take this 'Two Old Kings.' It has a lot more'n ten lines, but I don't care; they're short ones."

"All right," said Marjorie. "I'll choose 'The Merry Prince.' It has fourteen lines, but they're so gay and jolly, I think I can learn it pretty easy. What's yours, Kit?"

"I'll choose 'Ice Cream.' Partly 'cause I love it, and partly 'cause it's just ten lines."

"All right; now we'll fix the book," said King. "We'll put it on the floor, so. Now, Kit, your piece comes first, so you lie down, and stick your feet out that way, toward the window. Mops, your piece is 'most at the end of the book, so you sprawl out the other way. Mine is between, so I'll sneak in here, and I'll hold up the leaves for you girls."

The plan was not as complicated as it sounds, for the Maynards' favorite position for reading was lying prone, with the book open on the floor, and their heads supported by their hands.

But the three made a funny picture, as, quite oblivious of each other, they studied hard to learn the rhymes they had selected.

"Don't gabble out loud, Kit," begged her brother. "How can I study, when you're sissing 'Ice Cream, Ice Cream,' all the time?"

"All right, I'll study to myself," said Kitty, agreeably, and went on hissing her sibilant syllables in a whisper.

Marjorie stared into space, and studied without moving her lips, and King silently read his lines over and over, trusting to his "photographic memory" to retain them.

Miss Larkin peeped in, and seeing the absorbed students, kicking their heels or tapping their toes, went away again, unnoticed, but rejoicing that at least they were out of mischief.

"Hooray!" cried King, at last; "I know mine! I've said it over three times without looking."

"Go away, then," said Marjorie, her fingers in her ears, "until we know ours."

"All right; here, hold up these middle pages," and King left his sisters in possession of the book.

Kitty finished next, for Midget's lines turned out to be pretty hard ones to learn. But, after a while, they were firmly fixed in her curly head, and the three went in search of Miss Larkin.

"We're ready," King announced, cheerfully, as he offered her the book.

As they had found Miss Larkin in the pantry, and as she was just turning some jelly out of a mold—a proceeding which required extreme care—she did not extend a hearty welcome.

Moreover, the pantry, though roomy as a pantry, was not well adapted to the invasion of three eager and wide-awake children.

"Oh!" sighed Kitty, gazing rapturously at the laden shelves; "what beautiful desserty things! I thought you said only two people were coming, Miss Larkin."

In her zeal for entertainment, Miss Larkin had provided an over-abundance, and as she felt a little sensitive on the subject, Kitty's remark irritated her.

"Little girls shouldn't criticize their elders," she said, severely.

"Oh, I didn't mean to, Miss Larkin," cried Kitty, apologetically. "I'm sure I think the things are lovely. And prob'ly Mr. and Mrs. Mortimer have very large appetites."

"I hope they haven't," observed King; "I could eat most of these things myself. How about letting us try these little cakes, Miss Larkin?"

"Don't touch those!" was the rejoinder, as King's fingers hovered dangerously near the dainties; "that basket is filled, ready for the table. Come away from here. If you've learned your poems, I'll hear them, and then it's time for you to go and dress."

Miss Larkin pushed the reluctant children out of the fascinating pantry, and they all went to the library.

"Well, King," she said; "which is your poem?"

"Oh, let me say mine first," said Kitty, "'fore I forget it."

"You must have a short memory, child! Well, say yours first, then. Why, what sort of a book is this?"

"It's our scrap-book," explained Marjorie. "You didn't say what sort of poems, 'cept that they must be printed. So we took these. They're much more interesting than those in reg'lar books."

"Very well," said Miss Larkin, whose only intent had been to keep the children quiet for an hour. "Say yours first, then, Kitty."

So Kitty stood up, and with her hands behind her, recited her little jingle about

ICE CREAM.

I love to talk of my fav'rite theme,

So of course my subject is Ice Cream!

My Mother says that my eyes just beam

Whenever I even think Ice Cream!

When I've sewed a 'specially long, hard seam,

She takes me to town to get Ice Cream!

Sometimes the clouds in the blue sky seem

Like heaping saucers of white Ice Cream!

And often when I'm asleep, I dream

Of millions of platters of pink Ice Cream!

"You certainly know it perfectly, and you recite very nicely," said Miss Larkin. "Marjorie, you may say yours next."

"Mine is a jolly-sounding one," said Midget; "that's why I like it. It's called

"THE MERRY PRINCE."

50

The gay Prince Popinjay Peacock-Feather

Would play on his lute for hours together;

And feathery-weathery afternoons

He'd warble hilarious, various tunes.

He'd airily, merrily roam the street,

And sing to all he might chance to meet;

And if any were grumpy or gloomy or glum,

Along the Prince Peacock-Feather would come,

And sing them an affable, laughable lay,

Until they were gleeful, and glad, and gay,

They'd forget their bothers, and pothers, and wrongs,

When they listened to Popinjay's popular songs.

So let's be light-hearted, every one,

Like this frolicksome, rollicksome Prince of Fun!

"I don't wonder you like it," said Miss Larkin, smiling. "You're a Princess of Fun, yourself."

"So you are, Mopsy!" cried King. "I'll call you that, after this. Here goes for mine now, Miss Larkin, and then it's all over. Mine is one of those nonsense songs. Maybe you won't care for it, but we all love nonsense."

And then in an exaggerated declamatory style, and with dramatic gestures, Kingdon recited

TWO OLD KINGS.

Oh! the King of Kanoodledum

And the King of Kanoodledee,

They went to sea

In a jigamaree—

A full-rigged jigamaree.

51

And one king couldn't steer

And the other, no more could he;

    So they both upset

    And they both got wet—

As wet as wet could be.

And one king couldn't swim

And the other, he couldn't, too;

    So they had to float,

    While their empty boat

Danced away o'er the sea so blue.

Then the King of Kanoodledum

He turned a trifle pale,

    And so did he

    Of Kanoodledee,

But they saw a passing sail!

And one king screamed like fun

And the other king screeched like mad,

    And a boat was lowered

    And took them aboard;

And, My! but those kings were glad!

"I don't see much sense to it," admitted Miss Larkin, "but you have all done as I asked you to, and you've done it very nicely. Now you may each have a little cake, and then go and get dressed. And oh, children, do, please, be good while my visitors are here."

"We will, we truly will!" was the earnest reply.

CHAPTER IX
WILLING HELPERS

Very soon after half-past four, the Maynard quartette walked sedately into the drawing-room and seated themselves. Miss Larkin, herself just about to start for the station, regarded them critically.

"You look lovely," she declared, "all of you. And, beside being dressed prettily, you all look unusually good. In fact, I'm 'most afraid you look too good to be true! But you will keep yourselves tidy till we return, won't you? Don't romp, or pull off hair-ribbons."

"Touch those wonderful constructions!" exclaimed King, pointing to the unusually wide and elaborate bows that adorned the heads of his three sisters; "perish the thought! Nay! I will constitute myself chief protector of those marvels of headgear, and just as you see them now, so shall they stay to dazzle the eyes of the admiring Mortimers!"

When King declaimed in this highfalutin style, he was very funny, and even Miss Larkin smiled, though still a little anxious about their behavior.

"Well," she said, with a sigh, "I must go. I leave you in charge, King; you're the oldest. Can't you read aloud or do something to amuse yourselves quietly? If you don't, you'll get to tumbling around before you know it."

"Oh, we'll be good, Miss Larkin," declared Marjorie. "Skip along, now, or you'll be late at the train."

With a final glance round the pretty room, and at the pretty children, Miss Larkin went away.

"We'll give her a surprise," said Marjorie, as, from the window, she watched the carriage roll down the drive. "She really 'spects we're going to tear around and get all tumbled up 'fore she comes back. Now, let's be extra special careful to keep quiet and let her find us just as she left us."

"It's easy enough," agreed Kitty, "if you only make up your mind to it. But don't anybody read aloud—I hate it. If we want to read, let's read to ourselves."

"Don't read," said Midget, sociably; "let's just talk."

And so, perhaps unconsciously a little subdued by the atmosphere of the drawing-room, they sat quietly and conversed like model children.

Nurse Nannie looked in, and seeing all was well, left Rosy Posy with the others.

The baby, looking adorable in her dainty white frock, white socks and slippers, and white hair-ribbon, was perched demurely on a chair, holding one of her best dolls in her arms.

Midget, near the window, sometimes lifted the curtain a trifle to see if the returning carriage was yet in sight.

"They can't get here till five, Mopsy," said her brother; "and it's only twenty minutes to five now."

"I know it," said Midge; "but it always seems to hurry people up, if you look out the window for them."

"It doesn't, though," argued Kitty; "if they don't know you're looking."

"No," agreed Midget, amiably. Then she suddenly added, "Oh, King, look at all that smoke! It burst up all at once! Something is on fire!"

"I should say so!" cried King, going to the window. "Not very far away, either. Come out on the piazza."

"Fires are always farther away than they seem," said Kitty, as they went out at the front door and stood on the verandah, looking toward the smoke.

"Hullo, there's flame, too," said King. "Must be about as near as Bridge Street, anyhow. Let's go down to the gate."

Toward the gate they went, for what is so fascinating as a fire?

Kitty took Rosy Posy by the hand, and, mindful of their best clothes, the children didn't run, but walked quickly to the entrance of their own grounds.

"Where's the fire?" called King to a man who rushed by.

"Dunno," was the answer. "Summers down on Bridge Street, I guess. You can see from the corner."

So, of course, the Maynards went on to the corner of the block, from which point of vantage a much better view of the fire could be had.

It was a real conflagration, and no mistake. Smoke rose in volumes, and occasionally whirls of flame darted up through it. Never before had the children seen such a spectacle.

Thrilling with excitement, they went another block, and then some one passing them cried out, "Why, it's Simpson's old tumble-down house! Good thing for the town to have that go!"

"Oh, King!" cried Marjorie, her face white with horror, "it's Mrs. Simpson's house! How terrible! We must go and see if we can help them."

"Sure!" exclaimed King. "Why, Mr. Simpson's back in the hospital, you know. Whatever will she do, with all those children!"

The Simpsons were a poor family, who were special beneficiaries of the Maynards. Mr. Simpson, after an injury, had recovered sufficiently to leave the hospital, but a relapse had sent him back there again, and his wife, with seven children, had a hard time to get along at all. They lived in a large, but old and dilapidated, frame house in a poor quarter of the town.

Mr. and Mrs. Maynard had been very kind to them, and the Maynard children had often carried gifts of food or clothing to the needy family. Learning, then, that it was the Simpsons'

54

house that was burning, King and Marjorie started on a dead run, and Kitty followed, as fast as Rosy Posy's toddling steps would allow.

"Oh," cried Marjorie, as she ran; "the poor, dear people! I think only rich folks' houses ought to burn down, not poor widows', who haven't any other shelter."

"She isn't a widow," returned King, for he and Midget were running hand in hand.

"It's all the same," she responded. "Mr. Simpson is in the hospital, so she's as poor as a widow, anyway. We must do all we can to help them, King."

"'Course we must. If Father and Mother were only here, they'd do lots. We must do whatever they'd do."

By this time, they were nearing the burning house. A rather inefficient fire department was doing its best, but it was easily to be seen the whole house was doomed.

A crowd of men and boys were excitedly rushing about, jostling each other as they tried to save some of the furniture from the flames. But the broken and battered chairs and tables seemed scarcely worth saving, and their efforts were mostly expended in shouting orders to each other, which were never, by any chance, carried out.

Kingdon was indignant at their actions, and, throwing off his coat, began at once to lend whatever aid a fourteen-year-old boy could compass, and inspired by his enthusiasm, others began to do better work, and many of Mrs. Simpson's poor belongings were saved from destruction.

Marjorie went straight to the poor woman, herself, and found her sitting in a broken rocking-chair, with two children in her lap. She was watching the destruction of her forlorn home, and the tears ran down her pale cheeks, as she realized the magnitude of this, her latest disaster.

"There, there," said Marjorie, patting her shoulder, "don't cry so, Mrs. Simpson. Be thankful you and the children escaped with your lives. You might have all been burned to a black, you know!"

But this tragic suggestion was of no comfort.

"Better so, Miss," she replied, with fresh wails of grief. "Ah, yes, 'twould have been far better. Me, with me good man in the hospital, and seven homeless children, what can I ever do now?"

The question was, indeed, unanswerable, and the neighbors, many of them also poverty-stricken stood about volubly but uselessly sympathetic.

"Here, take these boxes, Mops," called King. "They're tied up, and they may have valuables in."

Marjorie took a pile of boxes from her brother, and Mrs. Simpson, looking at them with interest, said:

"Yes, I'm glad to save those; they're bits of ribbons and silks for patchwork."

As the poor woman had now no beds to put patchwork quilts on, the boxes did not seem so very valuable, but King hadn't waited to learn; he had returned to the house for other things. The firemen handed them out, or threw them from the windows, and those that King received he handed over to Marjorie and Kitty, who stacked them up in nondescript-looking heaps.

Kitty had stood Rosy Posy up against Mrs. Simpson, and bade her stay there.

"Look after her, please," she said to the half-distracted woman, "and then I can help save your things. Be good, won't you, Baby, and stay right there till sister comes back."

"Ess," acquiesced little Rosamond, and, sinking down on the ground, began to dig in the dirt with an iron spoon she found near by. Blissfully happy with this occupation, and pausing now and then to watch the novel spectacle of the burning house, Rosy Posy staid just where Kitty had told her, and Mrs. Simpson found it as easy to look after three babies as two.

The other five Simpson children were scattered among the crowd, the older ones realizing their misfortune, the others enjoying it as a new and startling form of entertainment.

"Well," said a fireman, as he rather perilously made his own escape from the falling walls, "there she goes! That's the last of her!" And then all that was left of the building collapsed into the flames, and nothing more of house or furniture could be saved.

For a few moments, everyone was silent, thrilled by the grandeur and awfulness of the sight, for there is always something awesome about uncontrollable flames.

Then the firemen turned their attention to extinguishing smouldering embers. Some of the neighbors started to go home, and others lingered out of curiosity, to see what the Simpsons would do.

"They'll have to go to the poorhouse," said one man, unfeelingly; "here comes the overseer now."

At sight of the overseer, and hearing the unsympathetic remark of the other, Mrs. Simpson's woe broke out afresh.

"The poorhouse for me!" she cried. "Me, who was a Foster! Oh, don't let me go there! I'll work me finger-ends off to keep a home for my childhern, somehow! Oh, if my man could be here with me! Have pity on a poor lone woman. Don't send me to the poorhouse."

"But what else can you do?" said the overseer of the poor. He was not unkindly in speech or tone, but he could see no other future for the mother and her seven children. Not one of them was old enough to earn a living, and as Mrs. Simpson had been in sore straits before the fire, surely she was really destitute now.

But the look of agony on her ashen face was so tragic that Marjorie felt her own heart breaking.

"Mrs. Simpson," she said, "you shall not go to the poorhouse! You shall come home with us!"

Everybody looked at the speaker in amazement. They all knew the Maynards, and had often had proofs of their kindness and generosity, but this declaration of Marjorie's took them by storm.

And Midget, as she stood before them, her tearful eyes spilling drops that made little furrows on her smoke-begrimed cheeks; her dainty white serge frock, soiled and ruined by her work of assistance; her hair-ribbon awry, but still rampant; seemed like an angel of mercy to the stricken woman, and the other auditors.

"Yes," she went on, "you shall go home with us, for a few days anyway, until we see what can be done. You and all the children shall at least have a roof to your head and a lamp to your feet."

Marjorie's enthusiasm was making her a little incoherent, and she looked appealingly at Kingdon. Loyalty to his sister stirred in the boy's soul, and as he saw a look of incredulity on some faces, he determined to stand by her amazing offer, although filled, himself, with secret consternation at the idea.

"Sure," he said, stepping to Marjorie's side, and taking her hand. "My father and mother are away, but I know they would do a heap for the Simpsons if they were at home. And Mother told us to do whatever she would approve of, so I know it's all right. We will take care of these stricken people"—this didn't sound quite right, but King hurried on—"and give them a home beneath a roof which hasn't yet burned down!"

It was characteristic of King to wax declamatory in exciting moments, and his loud tones, and the sight of the brother and sister standing nobly in their parents' place, so moved the audience, that they at once gave three cheers for the Maynards.

CHAPTER X
ON THE WAY HOME
Practical-minded Kitty was dismayed. She always looked ahead quicker and farther than Kingdon or Marjorie, and though her gentle little heart ached for the poor Simpsons, it would never have occurred to her to invite them into her own home.

But then, too, Kitty, as a younger sister, had always agreed to the plans of the older ones, unless by her common-sense she could argue them down. And in this instance there was no opportunity for argument. King and Midget had proved themselves heroes, and were even now receiving the applause that was their due. Since, therefore, the die was cast, Kitty had no intention of being left out of the glory of it.

Seizing Rosy Posy by the hand, the two ran to King's side, and the four Maynards received an ovation that would not have done discredit to a returning war-veteran.

To be sure, the admiring audience was largely composed of the citizens of this lowly locality, but their appreciation was as deep and their voices were as strong as those of the aristocrats on the other side of the bridge.

"And as we're going to do this," said Kitty, when the cheers had subsided, "we'd better get about it before all those children catch their death of cold."

It was five o'clock now, and the sun was getting low, and the March wind high.

The seven small Simpsons had on no hats or wraps, nor, for that matter, did the four small Maynards, so Kitty's suggestion was really on the side of wisdom and prudence.

"Right you are, little Miss," said the burly overseer, "and as you children are so kind as to take these sufferin' folks to your own house, I'll see to it that what few sticks of furnicher they've saved is taken care of."

"Oh, thank you!" cried Marjorie; "then we can go right home. I'm so afraid our baby will catch cold. And Mrs. Simpson's babies, too," she added, considerately. "Come on, Rosy Pet; come with Middy."

Rosamond put her cold little hand in Midget's, and Kitty said, "We must all run; that's the way to get warm. Come on."

"Wait a minute," said Mrs. Simpson, who had not yet really accepted her invitation; "I'm thinkin' it ain't right for us to go to your ma's house, an' her away from home. It ain't for the likes of us to go into a grand house with carpets and pictures. And I'm thinkin' we'd ought to go to the poorhouse, after all."

For a moment Marjorie felt relieved. After her impulsive invitation, a sort of reaction had left her wondering how it would all turn out. And now she had a chance to retract and reconsider her offer.

But again the woebegone look on Mrs. Simpson's tearful face, and the forlornness of the seven shivering children smote her heart, and she couldn't help saying:

"It is right, Mrs. Simpson. You know how kind my mother is to you, and now she's away, I'm head of the house."

Unconsciously, Marjorie drew up her plump little figure to its full height, and her air of authority carried its own conviction.

"Yes, indeed," chimed in King. "And I know my father would say just what I say; come ahead, Mrs. Simpson, and welcome!"

As a matter of fact, King was not moved so much by the certainty that his father would say this, as by his natural impulse to back up Marjorie's invitation, and also assert his own position as "head of the house" equally with herself.

Something of this same spirit imbued Kitty, and she said:

"Indeed, I think we'd be very selfish not to share our home with these poor, afflicted people. Mrs. Simpson, don't you bother about anything at all; you just bring your children and come right along with us. Father often says to us, 'Children, in a 'mergency you must think for yourselves, and think quickly.' So now we've thought, and we did it as quick as we could; so you just come on and say no more about it."

Kitty did not mean to be crisp of speech, but Mrs. Simpson was still looking uncertain, and diffidently hanging back, and Kitty was anxious to get home.

"Yes; come on," said King, realizing himself the need for immediate action.

"Well, I'll go, just for to-night," said Mrs. Simpson, looking scared at her own decision. "I'll go, as I haven't a roof where to lay my head—I mean—a—a———"

The poor woman was really incoherent from shock and excitement. Always frail, she had overworked her strength to keep her family clothed and fed, and now she was nearly at the end of her endurance.

"Here, ma'am, I'll go with you," said a kind-hearted neighbor, one of the few now left in the rapidly thinning crowd. He took the poor woman by the arm, saying, "You Simpson children come along, now," and then waited respectfully for the Maynards to lead the way. So King marched boldly ahead, followed by Midget and Kitty, with the tired Rosy Posy between them. Next came Mrs. Simpson and her escort, and then the seven Simpson children, shy and awkward now, by reason of a sudden realization of where they were going.

It was far from being an imposing-looking parade. Kingdon, though valiant-hearted, was secretly a little dubious about the whole proceeding. It had been Marjorie's idea, and he had willingly subscribed to it, but it certainly was a great responsibility.

It was right—yes, he felt sure it was right—but it seemed to open up such a bewildering array of future consequences, that he couldn't even dare to think about them.

Then suddenly he realized that he was lonely. Why should he walk alone? He turned to join the other three, feeling the necessity of sympathetic companionship, but at the sight of the three girls behind him, he burst into a peal of laughter.

"Oh! if you could see yourselves!" he cried, for he hadn't before noticed their appearance. "Mops, you're just covered with smoky smudges—your dress is more black than white! And Kit, how did you get torn so?"

The girls stood still and looked at each other. Never before in their short lives, had they been through an occasion so momentous as to render them entirely oblivious of everything else. But the fire and its thrilling scenes, followed by this absorbing responsibility of the Simpsons' entire career, had left them no time to think of themselves or each other.

"Goodness gracious me!" exclaimed Marjorie, as she looked at the awful wrecks of her two sisters' once immaculate costumes; "am I as bad as that?"

"Your face is even blacker than Kit's," declared King, after looking critically at each. "Rosy Posy, you seem to have met a waterspout somewhere."

"Ess," said the little one, forlornly. "Nassy old big man frowed water on me out o' a long hose fing."

It was quite evident that a careless fireman had deluged the child, and King looked greatly concerned.

"She'll get pneumonia in those wet clothes," he said; "we must hurry home faster. Come, Baby, brother'll carry you."

"Do, p'ease," she said; "I'se so tired an' wet."

A chubby five-year-old is no light burden for a boy, but King picked up his little sister, and trudged on faster.

"Oh, King!" said Marjorie, hurrying her steps to keep up with him, "I've just thought of it! The Mortimers will be there when we get home!"

"I've thought of it all along," said King, with a gloomy shake of his head. "I don't know what'll happen, Mops; but we've got to brave it out now."

"But how can we? What will Miss Larkin say?"

"You ought to have thought of that sooner," said Kitty. "I did. I thought of her first thing. But you two didn't ask my advice."

Poor Kitty couldn't help this little fling. Often her judgment was better than theirs, but being older, King and Marjorie never asked her opinion until it was too late.

"And think how we look!" wailed Marjorie, her mind going ahead, as they neared home.

"I've been thinking of it," said King, grimly, as he shifted the baby to his other arm. "I say, Mops, we're in no end of a mess, and I don't know what we're up against. But there's one comfort; it isn't mischief, and we haven't done anything wrong."

"It isn't mischief," agreed Midget; "that's sure. But I'm not so sure we haven't done wrong. When I asked Mrs. Simpson, it seemed the only thing to do; and it seemed—it seemed——"

"Grand and noble," suggested King.

"Yes, it did! Sort of splendid, and 'love thy neighbor as thyself,' you know. But now——"

"Now," said Kitty, "we've got to face the music. We've got to go in the house, looking like ragpickers ourselves, and taking with us a crowd of people who look—well, nearly as bad! and then, we've got to face Miss Larkin and her grand company!"

"We can't!" exclaimed Marjorie, stopping short, quite appalled at the picture Kitty drew so graphically.

"We've got to!" declared King. "Come on, Mops, I can't carry this baby much farther. Rosy Posy, you're a bunch of sweetness, but you're an awful heavy one."

"Is I?" said the little one, apologetically, as she nestled close to the big brother whom she adored, and patted his grimy face with her equally grimy little hand.

"Let me carry the little girl," said the big man, who, just behind, was looking after Mrs. Simpson.

But Rosamond was shy, and utterly refused to go to the arms of a stranger.

"Never mind," said King, wearily. "We're almost home now. I can manage her."

They turned in at the front gate, and the procession started up the Maynard driveway.

"Guess I'll go back now," said the stranger man, a little abashed at the sight of the great house, brilliantly lighted, that was partly visible through the trees. "You all right, now, Mis' Simpson?"

"Yes," said the trembling woman, frightened herself, and weak from fatigue and exhaustion.

"Here, you Sam," said the man to the oldest boy; "come here and take a-hold of your ma. She's pretty near faintin'. Get her to bed's soon's you can. Good-bye, all!"

With an embarrassed gesture, he snatched off his old cap, replaced it as suddenly, and turning, fled down the path in an actual spasm of stage-fright.

Though Mrs. Simpson had not heard the children's discussion on the way home, he had, and he knew that warm-hearted as the little Maynards were, they had a serious situation confronting them when they opened their own front door.

This, and his own embarrassment at the sight of unaccustomed grandeur, made him seek refuge in panic-stricken flight.

Some of the young Simpsons were almost ready to follow him, but the braver ones were on tiptoe of glad expectation at the thought of going into the beautiful house. They knew the Maynards pretty well, and having always found them kindly and pleasant, had no fear save such as was engendered by the awe of wealth and luxurious surroundings.

"Set down the baby, and let me think a minute," said Marjorie to her brother, as they were within a few yards of the house. "We've got to take the Simpsons in, of course, but do you think Miss Larkin would like it better if we all went round to the side door? You see, we all look like the dickens, and she's so particular about those Mortimer people."

"No, I don't think so," said King. "This is an emergency. It's an accident, a tragedy, a very special occasion. She will have to forgive our appearance, 'cause we couldn't help it. We were doing our best to be helpful to people in trouble, and if we got all messed up by it, it isn't our fault. And, besides, it's our house, and the Simpsons are our comp'ny. We've more right there than Miss Larkin and her comp'ny. So, if she has any sense, she'll understand all this. And so, I say, go right in the front door, and do our best."

"I think all that, too," agreed Midge, "but I only thought if it would hurt Larky's feelings to see us girls looking so disreputable, we might spruce into clean clothes before we saw the Mortimers."

"What do you think, Kit?" said King, with a sudden remembrance of Kitty's good sense in a dilemma.

Kitty, much elated at being appealed to, answered at once:

"I think King's right. It's our house, and this is our whole show. Miss Larkin has company to-night, and that's her whole show. We needn't interfere with each other at all. 'Course it's too bad that we look so dirty and all, but who wouldn't, after they'd been managing a whole fire? And so I say, let's march right in, and not act as if we'd been doing anything wrong. We haven't, and I don't see, Mops, why you act as if we had."

"It isn't wrong," said Marjorie, still standing still, and digging her patent-leather toe thoughtfully into the hard ground of the drive; "but I do want to spare Larky's feelings all I can. She was so particular about our keeping clean, and you know, we truly meant to, and now, look at us!"

"Oh, pshaw!" said Kitty; "we'd have kept lovely and clean if we'd stayed at home. But we went out, and got into this—this predickerment, and 'course we got smoky and all. We can get washed and dressed after we tell Larky all about it. Come on, do; I'm awful hungry, and I'm tired, too."

"All right," said Marjorie, still a little doubtful; "come on, then. You can walk now, can't you, Posy Pet?"

"Ess; I's all wested now. Take hold my hand."

So the four Maynards, hand in hand, walked on, and then mounted the broad steps of their own front verandah.

"Come on, Mrs. Simpson," said Marjorie, over her shoulder. Her voice was full of the kindest hospitality and welcome. In doubt about Miss Larkin's attitude in the matter, she might be; in doubt about the wisdom of making their entrance before strange guests, without first repairing their toilets, she might be; but in Marjorie's honest little heart there was not a shadow of doubt that she was doing right in offering the shelter of her home to these unfortunate refugees.

She felt sure that had her parents been at home they would have done the same thing, and in their absence her own sense of responsibility asserted itself, and upheld her in her present action.

The eight Simpsons trudged up the steps behind the Maynards, and as they all stood in front of the long glass doors, whose heavy lace panels only partly screened the brightly lighted hall, King rang the bell.

CHAPTER XI
A FRIEND IN NEED
Now, while the Simpsons' cottage had been burning, the occupants of the Maynard house had been in a state of great consternation. Miss Larkin and her two guests from Boston had arrived shortly after five o'clock, and Sarah met them at the door with a scared look on her face.

"Are the children with you, ma'am?" she said, as Miss Larkin stepped across the threshold.

"With me, Sarah? No, indeed. I left them in the drawing-room."

"Well, they're not there, ma'am; and they're not in the house. I thought as how they must have run out to meet the carriage. Master King's cap and the little girls' hats is in their places, so they haven't gone far."

"Oh, I suppose they're hiding, to tease us," said Miss Larkin, in an annoyed tone. "They'll probably jump out of the guest-room wardrobe, or something like that. Mrs. Mortimer, you must be prepared for childish pranks. The little Maynards are the most mischievous children I ever saw."

Mrs. Mortimer smiled, and said nothing, but her expression seemed to indicate little tolerance for juvenile misbehavior. She had no children of her own, and so had not learned patience and forbearance as mothers have to.

But Mr. Mortimer was by nature more sympathetic with childish ways.

"Good for the kiddies!" he cried. "I like little folks with some fun in them. If they jump out of a cupboard at me, they'll catch a rousing reception."

He smiled broadly, and looked about for some laughing faces to appear suddenly.

"It's nice of you to be so indulgent," said Miss Larkin, but she herself was far from pleased. She had hoped to present four demure and prettily-dressed children, whose manners should seem above reproach even to exacting Mrs. Mortimer.

However, there was no sight or sound of the Maynard quartette, so the guests were shown to their rooms by Sarah, while Miss Larkin laid aside her own wraps, and then went to the kitchen to see that dinner was progressing properly.

"Where do you suppose the children are, Ellen?" she asked of the cook.

The good-natured face of the Irishwoman looked a little anxious, as she replied:

"Shure, I dunno, ma'am. I'm thinkin' it's not hidin' they do be, fer they'd be fer bowsin' out afore this. No, Miss Larkin, they must 'ave went out to meet the kerridge, an' thin, their attintion bein' divarted, they've wint som'ers else."

"Oh, nonsense, Ellen; they wouldn't go off like that, without hats, and with their best clothes on."

"It's no sayin' what them childher wud or wuddent do, ma'am. There's nothin' I'd put past 'em; nothin' at all, ma'am!"

"Well, but, Ellen—if they're not in the house—if they've wandered away, we ought to send some one after them. It's dark now, and they should be at home."

"An' where wud ye be sindin' to, ma'am? Shure they might be over to Mis' Spencer's—I jist thought o' that."

"I'll telephone over and find out. Meanwhile, go on with the preparations for dinner, Ellen; I still think they're hiding in the house, the naughty little rascals."

Greatly annoyed at the troublesome situation, Miss Larkin telephoned to Mrs. Spencer, and to one or two other neighbors, but could get no word of the children.

Then, hearing her guests coming downstairs, she returned to the drawing-room to receive them.

63

"I can't understand it," she said, as they came in; "if the children were hiding, they would appear by this time. They are not the kind to keep still very long. The cook thinks they are not in the house, but Sarah and I think they must be."

"Jolly little scamps!" said Mr. Mortimer, rubbing his hands in glee. "When I was a child, I always loved to play practical jokes myself."

"I didn't," said Mrs. Mortimer, as she seated herself stiffly on the satin sofa. "I think it very bad manners, and I'm surprised that Helen Maynard encourages such ways in her children."

"Well, I must say it isn't Helen's fault," said Miss Larkin, eager to do her friend justice; "Helen is really pretty strict with them, in her gentle way. But they are everlastingly inventing some new kind of mischief that no one ever heard of before. Like as not, they are out on the roof, or in some such crazy place."

"The roof!" gasped Mrs. Mortimer, raising her hands in horror. "Won't they fall off?"

"Oh, they're not really there," said Miss Larkin, "and they wouldn't fall off if they were. But I don't know exactly what to do. I can't help feeling worried about them. Suppose they've all been kidnapped."

"Kidnappers don't often take four at a time," said Mr. Mortimer, smiling. "I fancy they're all right, wherever they are."

It was at this moment the doorbell rang.

It did not occur to Miss Larkin that the children might be outside, and seating herself primly, she waited while Sarah admitted the guest, whoever it might be.

So Sarah opened the front door, and at sight of the four untidy-looking children, and the nondescript group behind them, she gave an uncontrollable shriek, and fell back, half-dazed, as what seemed like an endless procession of people marched in.

King and Marjorie, as ringleaders, went straight up to Miss Larkin.

"We brought these people home with us," explained Marjorie, simply. "They are the Simpsons. Their house burned down, and their father is in the hospital, and they have no home to cover their heads, and so we brought them here. Father and Mother always look out for them and——"

But Marjorie quailed at last before the flush of anger on Miss Larkin's face, and the look of frozen horror on the countenance of the strange lady, who, she knew, must be Mrs. Mortimer.

Suddenly she realized her own shocking appearance, and the dreadful spectacle of the crowd behind her.

But Kingdon rose to the occasion.

"And so, Miss Larkin," he went on, slipping his comforting hand into Midget's, "as Mopsy and I have to take Father and Mother's place while they're away, we invited Mrs. Simpson and her children to come here for a few days, until they get another home."

"Here! A few days!" repeated Miss Larkin, and, looking helplessly about, she sank back into the chair from which she had risen, and, closing her eyes, seemed about to faint away.

"Ugh! how appalling!" said Mrs. Mortimer, in the tone one might use at seeing a dozen boa constrictors suddenly turned loose in one's vicinity.

But there was also a note of contempt in her voice, which touched Marjorie's self-respect. At any rate, she must not forget her own manners, whatever Miss Larkin's guest might do. She turned to the strange lady, and curtseyed prettily.

"How do you do, Mrs. Mortimer?" she said; "I can't shake hands until I'm tidied up."

"I should think not," said Mrs. Mortimer, with a slight shudder, but Marjorie, having made her greetings, turned to the other guest.

She was about to speak to him in the same formal manner, when he grasped her hand, and said, cordially:

"How do you do, Miss Marjorie? You have evidently had an adventure. Can I help you in any way?"

His genial tones as well as his actual words were such a comfort to Marjorie, that she regained at once her rapidly-disappearing composure, and felt that she had found, most unexpectedly, a helpful friend.

King, too, appreciated the gentleman's good-will, and after a few words of greeting, felt his own courage fortified, and went over to where Miss Larkin sat, with her eyes still closed to the dreadful sight before her. "Now, look here, Larky," he whispered, "you're making it all worse by acting like that. Brace up to the 'casion, and let's see what we can do."

"What we can do!" echoed Miss Larkin, as she opened her eyes to treat Kingdon to an angry glare. "There's nothing to do! You have disgraced me forever."

"Indeed you have," said Mrs. Mortimer, who seemed to resent the invasion quite as much as if she were, herself, in authority. "I have heard you children were mischievous, but I never could have dreamed of such a high-handed performance as this."

"But it had to be high-handed," urged Kitty, who took the guest's speech very seriously. "There was no time for anything but a high-handed performance. Why, you know how fast a fire burns——" she said, turning to Mr. Mortimer, as to the one friend in sight.

"Indeed, I do," he responded, heartily. "And now, that this rather unexpected event has occurred, some of its minor details must be attended to."

The Maynards, despite their anxiety and worry, looked at Mr. Mortimer with open-eyed curiosity. They were not surprised at the attitudes of Miss Larkin and Mrs. Mortimer, but for a complete stranger to enter so into the spirit of their own intent, and, moreover, to have a lurking twinkle in his eye, that spoke well for his sense of humor, was, indeed, cheering.

"Yes, sir; that's just it," said Kitty, delighted to find some one who appreciated the need for immediate action. "We've asked these people here, and now we must provide for them." She clasped her sooty little hands, as she looked confidently up into the kind face that smiled quizzically at her.

"Yes, that is so," Mr. Mortimer agreed. And then he turned to Miss Larkin, who was still unable to cope with the situation.

"It seems to me," he said, looking at his wife and his hostess, who were both fairly helpless with indignation, "that, if you will permit me, Miss Larkin, I will advise and assist the Maynard children in this rather trying matter. I am not surprised that you are a little overcome, and so at risk of seeming presumptuous, I am going to do all I can to bring about a more satisfactory state of affairs."

"James," said Mrs. Mortimer, "I think you are overstepping all bounds of propriety. I think that neither you nor Miss Larkin are called upon to interfere in this dreadful escapade of Mrs. Maynard's children. Summon the servants, and let them do whatever may be necessary."

Marjorie flushed crimson. She felt that a guest of Miss Larkin had no right to talk so about other guests who had been invited to the Maynard house by the Maynards themselves. But she also knew that a little girl must not express views contrary to those of a grown-up lady, so she said nothing.

"There, there, Hester," said her husband, "don't put your finger in this pie. One of our family is enough, and I propose to do all the interfering myself. Now, Kingdon and Marjorie, as I know nothing of your household, I'll have to ask a few questions. Where did you propose to put these guests of yours to sleep to-night?"

"I don't know what Midget thought," said King, "and I hadn't quite settled it in my own mind; but I thought Ellen or James would help us out. There's an extra room in the attic that Mrs. Simpson could use, and then—I thought maybe James could fix some bunks somewhere for the children."

"Yes," said Marjorie, "there's a big loft over the carriage-house——"

"But that's too cold," objected Kitty. "I thought they could sleep in the kitchen."

"The kitchen!" exclaimed Mrs. Mortimer, in that tone of biting sarcasm that was even more irritating than Miss Larkin's dumb despair.

Meantime the household servants, though they had not been summoned, were hovering round in the hall.

Ellen, at risk of endangering the fine dinner she was preparing, had come to see if she could help her beloved young people in any way. Nannie, seeing Rosy Posy's plight, had carried her off to the nursery, and Sarah, wringing her hands in dismay, was consulting in whispers with Thomas, as to what could be done to help Miss Marjorie and Master King out of this scrape.

As for the Simpsons themselves, they, of course, had no part in the discussion. Mrs. Simpson, in a sort of apathy, sat with her head drooped, and a baby in her arms; while two others, scarcely more than babies, clutched at her dress and hid their faces if any one looked at them. The other four stood behind their mother's chair, wriggling awkwardly, and uncertain whether to cry or to feel pleased at being guests of the great house, even though of doubtful welcome.

"No, Miss Kitty, dear," said Ellen, coming to the doorway of the drawing-room, "ye can't be afther usin' my kitchen fer bedrooms. But the pore woman can have my bed fer the night, an' I'll shlape on the flure or annywhere, so I will."

"An' I will, too," said Sarah, wiping her eyes, for her warm heart sympathized with the anxiety of the children she loved.

"An' I'll see to some few of 'em," said Thomas, from the background, "though I'm sure, Miss Marjorie, they'd all catch pewmonia a-sleepin' in the carriage-loft."

"Now, I'll make a suggestion," said Mr. Mortimer. "Ellen, do you think you could make Mrs. Simpson and that smallest baby comfortable for the night?"

"I'm shure I cud, sor."

"Very well. Take her away at once. Give her a cup of tea, and some supper, and then send her to bed. The poor soul is quite worn out, and no wonder."

Realizing the authority of the strange gentleman, Ellen took Mrs. Simpson's arm, and without another word, the two went away, the mother carrying with her the youngest child.

"Now," went on Mr. Mortimer, "I next dismiss the three Maynards to a liberal use of soap and water. Don't spare the soap; use sand, if necessary. But get yourselves clean and—I suppose you have other clothes?"

"Yes, sir," serious Kitty assured him.

"Then get them on, as expeditiously as possible. And with the assistance of Thomas, I will assume the management of these six remaining Simpsons. Run away, now, ask no questions, but leave all to me."

King and Midget felt as if a weight were lifted from their shoulders. It did not seem like ignobly shifting a responsibility, for Mr. Mortimer left them no choice in the matter. He gave commands evidently with the intention of having them obeyed.

And so, with a very earnest squeeze of his hand, Marjorie obeyed his decree, and went upstairs, with King and Kitty on either side of her.

"Well, if he isn't a trump!" she cried, as they reached the upper hall.

"Brick!" declared King.

"Yes, he is," agreed Kitty, thoughtfully. "Except Father, nobody could be as nice as he is."

"Nobody!" echoed the other two.

"And now," said Marjorie, "let's do the best we can to get dressed quick, and get downstairs in time for dinner. Let's put on our best clothes, and our best manners, and perhaps that crosspatch lady will like us a little better."

67

"She never will!" sighed Kitty, with conviction. "She hates us."

"Oh, let's get round her," said King hopefully. "If we're lovely and sweet and pleasant, she'll have nothing to growl at."

"And clean," supplemented Kitty. "If you look in the mirror, you'll see one reason why she was so disgusted."

"Yes," laughed King; "and if you girls look in the mirror, you'll see two reasons!"

Midge and Kitty were truly scandalized when they saw their mirrored selves, and were glad of Nurse Nannie's helpful hands to restore tidiness.

Rosy Posy was already bathed and tucked in her crib, where she sat up against a pillow, eating bread and milk with a sleepy disregard of the afternoon's excitement.

And so, it was not more than half an hour later when three spick and span Maynards went downstairs again, in fresh attire, from hair-ribbons to slipper-bows, though, of course, King didn't wear hair-ribbons.

CHAPTER XII
THE HOUSE ON SPRUCE STREET
In the drawing-room they found only the two ladies.

Perhaps Mr. Mortimer had asked them to treat the children with more kindliness, and perhaps they themselves concluded they had been too harsh in their judgment, but at any rate, their reception was far less chilly than it had been an hour ago.

Mrs. Mortimer was positively gracious in her demeanor, and even smiled as she gave Marjorie her finger-tips, after the little girl had made her best curtsey.

Kitty followed, and King, though he had to fight down his resentful feelings, behaved with the winsome politeness which always characterized his "good manners."

The children were consumed with curiosity to know how the Simpsons had been disposed of, but deemed it better to ask no questions. So the conversation was on trivial subjects, and Miss Larkin grew quite amiable, as she realized that, though belated, this was the scene into which she had desired to introduce her guest. The Simpson subject was ignored, until, just before dinner was announced, Mr. Mortimer returned, his eyes twinkling, and his whole expression betokening great amusement.

They went to the dining-room then, and not until the soup had been served, did he satisfy the children's eager desire to know what had happened.

"I think I owe it to you, Miss Marjorie," he began, "to tell you what I did with your guests."

"Oh, if you please, Mr. Mortimer," said Marjorie, with shining eyes.

"Well, you see, it was a hard nut to crack," he went on, unable to resist delaying the tale in order to tease them a little bit. "There were six children, all of them hungry, tired, and sleepy. To feed them here, would have been a great tax on your servants, especially as you already had house-guests. I found that this town of yours, progressive as it is, has no orphan asylum, and besides, the Simpsons aren't orphans, anyway."

"What did you do?" cried Kitty, unable to conceal her interest.

"Why," said Mr. Mortimer, slowly, as one who knows he is about to create a sensation, "Why, I put them up at the hotel."

"What!" cried his wife and Miss Larkin in unison, while Kitty looked incredulous, King shouted in glee, and Marjorie giggled.

"Yes," went on Mr. Mortimer, "it was really the only thing to do. It was that, or the Police Station——and I'm not sure there is a police station in Rockwell. It seems to be a very small town, and without some of the institutions of a metropolis. But it boasts a fair-sized hotel, which, fortunately, is not over-crowded at the present time."

King chuckled at this, for the scarcity of patronage at the "Rockwell House" was a local joke.

"And did you really put them there, as regular customers?" asked Marjorie, unable to believe such a proceeding possible.

"Well, I don't know about regular customers; indeed, the landlord seemed to think the whole deal a little irregular. But, anyway, they're there for the night."

"The Simpson children, at a hotel!" cried King, nearly choking in his attempt to restrain his laughter.

And indeed, so incongruous was the idea, after having seen the young people in question, that even Mrs. Mortimer smiled, while Miss Larkin laughed in spite of herself.

"Oh!" said Kitty, whose vivid imagination pictured the scene, "I wish I had been there! Did you register them?"

This suggestion sent King and Midget into chuckles again, and Mr. Mortimer said, gravely:

"Of course I did; from Samuel down to Mary Eliza. And I fancy those six names will always be pointed to with pride by the worthy proprietor."

"I hope, sir," said King, suddenly remembering his position as "man of the house," "that you directed him to send the bill to my father."

"I'll tell you what I did do," said Mr. Mortimer, with a business-like air that somehow made King feel very manly at being thus addressed: "I told him the circumstances of the case. I told him of your generous offer of hospitality, and of the difficulties in the way of entertaining the whole Simpson family at your own home. I laid before him the fact that the town ought to take some interest in this calamity that has befallen one of its poorer families; and we finally arranged that he was to make his charges as moderate as possible, that Mr. Maynard would be responsible for half the bill, and that the city authorities should be asked to pay the other half. All of this, of course, subject to your father's sanction; and agreed to by us, in order to meet the emergency."

"You did fine!" exclaimed King. "Thank you, Mr. Mortimer. I know Father will say you did just right—unless he prefers to pay the whole bill himself."

"He can do as he likes about that. He can settle the matter with the city authorities. But the hotel man—a mighty sensible chap, by the way—seemed to think the townspeople would stand quite ready to do their share, both individually and as a public measure."

"I think they will," said Marjorie, "for I remember when Mr. Simpson first went to the hospital, the town looked after the family, or something—I don't know just what, but I know we only helped."

"And so," concluded Mr. Mortimer, "the small Simpsons are to-night enjoying the luxury of lodging in a hotel, whatever fate may bring them to-morrow."

"You have been very kind," said Marjorie, her eyes fairly brimming with gratitude. "I don't know what we should have done if you hadn't been here."

"You would have had more room in your own house," said Mr. Mortimer, smiling.

But Miss Larkin said, "Indeed we wouldn't have put those children in our pretty guest rooms."

"I don't know," said Kitty; "I think we would have had to do so. For I'm sure it never would have occurred to us to take them to the hotel!"

Again King shook with laughter.

"I'd like to see them," he said; "imagine those scared-to-death youngsters, sitting up in the hotel dining-room!"

"Is there anybody to look after them?" asked Miss Larkin. "A matron, or anybody?"

"Well, of course, it isn't a juvenile asylum," said Mr. Mortimer; "but I persuaded the landlord's wife to take an interest in the poor little scraps of humanity. They really seemed very lonesome and forlorn."

"I don't think they need to," observed Kitty. "They're much more comfortable, by this time, than they've ever been before in their lives. I don't believe they ever have enough to eat, except when we take them Christmas dinners or Thanksgiving baskets."

"Poor things!" exclaimed Miss Larkin, who was exceedingly sympathetic, now that her dinner party was no longer interfered with. "To-morrow, we must see what we can do for them."

"Do," said Mrs. Mortimer; "I'm sorry for them, I'm sure. But now let's talk of more agreeable matters."

It seemed to Marjorie that the Boston lady was a bit heartless, but as the children were not expected to take much part in the conversation anyway, they behaved beautifully during the rather lengthy dinner, and thought out little plans of their own, while their elders were talking.

After dinner, they were excused, and, rather relieved at not being expected to go in the drawing-room again, they went upstairs.

70

They congregated for a few moments in the playroom, before going to bed, and discussed hastily some plans for the next day.

"I do think Mr. Mortimer was just lovely," said Midget. "He makes up for his wife. She hasn't any heart at all, I don't b'lieve she'd have cared if this house had burned up, 'stead of the Simpsons'!"

"Never mind her, Mopsy," put in King; "'tisn't polite to jump on guests that way! But I tell you, girls, to-morrow we'll stir up the town. I didn't know that they ought to look after people that get burned out, but we'll see that they do."

"How?" queried Kitty, who loved to plan.

"Well, we'll go and see that landlord man at the hotel, first. He'll tell us what to do, I guess. You know, we oughtn't to bother Mr. Mortimer any further in the matter."

"All right," said Marjorie, yawning; "and I'm awful sleepy, King. Let's settle it all in the morning."

"All right; good-night, girls," and with a brotherly tweak at their curls, being careful not to pull their "dress-up" hair-ribbons, he was off to his own room.

Next morning, Marjorie came downstairs, ready for action.

It was Saturday, so there was no school, and the three Maynards decided to devote the day to seeing what they could do in aid of the Simpson family.

Mr. Mortimer smiled, when they thanked him over and over for his kindness of the night before, and then excused him from any further responsibility in the matter.

"Oho!" said he, "am I to be left out of this picnic?"

"It isn't exactly a picnic," said Kitty, "and we thought you'd rather be left out."

"You've already done so much," said King, "I'm sure we couldn't expect you to do anything more. Besides, Miss Larkin says you're all going driving this morning."

"Yes, we are," said his hostess. "I want to show you round this part of the country. Some of the drives are beautiful."

Mr. Mortimer made a comical face at the children, as if to say he was not master of his fate, and must do as he was bid, and then they all went to breakfast.

While at the table, Marjorie was called to the telephone.

Mr. Adams, the father of Dorothy, talked to her, and told her that Mr. Jennings, of the hotel, had told him the whole story.

"And, Marjorie," he said, "I am quite willing to let the Simpsons have that cottage of mine round on Spruce Street for a few months, anyway. It isn't large, but it's in good repair, and they're welcome to the use of it for a time."

71

"Oh, how good you are!" exclaimed Midget. "And what about furniture, Mr. Adams?"

"Well, my wife, and a few other ladies, are already talking that matter over. They think that many of our citizens will contribute some beds, chairs, and tables; and so, if you have any discarded things like that in your attic, you may donate them. But don't give anything your mother might want to keep."

"All right," returned Marjorie. "I'll go over to see Mrs. Adams after breakfast, and we'll see what we can do."

Midget felt very grown up at being consulted by Mr. Adams, and it was with an air of importance that she returned to the breakfast table. She told of Mr. Adams' kindness in letting the Simpsons use his vacant house, which was really a pretty little cottage on a pleasant street.

"Whew!" said King, "they'll have to brace up if they're going to live in a house like that. Why, it's an awful jolly little place."

"It may be a good thing for them," said Mr. Mortimer. "Teach them self-respect, and help them to try to keep their heads up."

"Won't it be fun to fix it up for them!" exclaimed Marjorie. "I shall give them my old bureau cover—my new one is nearly finished."

"Ho!" said King; "they need lots of things much more than a bureau cover. Let's ask Mr. Smith, the grocer, to give them a barrel of flour."

"Don't strike too high," advised Mr. Mortimer; "ask him for a sack of flour, and you're more likely to get it. Why don't you children canvass the town? I'm sure you could wheedle more charity out of the shopkeepers and other citizens than all the city authorities together."

"I'd like to," said Marjorie, dubiously, "but I don't know whether Father would approve of that. Once we were a Village Improvement Society, and we got into an awful fuss!"

"But that was quite different," urged Kitty. "This is for charity—a noble cause. I'd just as lieve go round with a basket, and collect things for them."

"Not literally a basket, my child," advised Mr. Mortimer, "but surely it would do no harm to ask contributions from the people you know well."

"I'll tell you what!" exclaimed King. "Let the whole Jinks Club do it. We never have done anything charitable in the Club, and this is a good time to begin."

"Well," said Marjorie, "I think it would be fine. But let's go and ask Mrs. Adams about it first. I guess she's at the head of the Poor Society, and she'll tell us what to do."

So, after breakfast, the three Maynard "Jinkses" started out. They gathered in Delight on the way, and while the girls went to Dorothy's house, King ran over for Flip Henderson.

Mrs. Adams not only approved their plan, but offered to loan a big wagon, a pair of horses, and a driver to transport any furniture or clothing that might be donated.

Then such fun as the Jinks Club had! They called on everybody they knew, and some that they didn't know. They collected a fine lot of second-hand furniture, and clothing, as well as a liberal supply of provisions. Two or three kind-hearted people donated coal and wood; and though many of the contributors sent their gifts themselves, yet some had no means of doing so, and Mrs. Adams' wagon carried many loads to the cottage on Spruce Street.

The Maynards went home to luncheon, jubilant.

"Such fun!" they cried, as they bounded in at the front door. "We've loads of things already in the house, and what do you think, Miss Larkin—the bureau that Mrs. Chester gave, exactly fits my bureau cover! Isn't that fine?"

So enthusiastic were the children at luncheon, that Miss Larkin and Mrs. Mortimer were interested before they knew it.

"I'd like to go over and see the house," said Mrs. Mortimer, at last. "I really think you young people have done wonders."

"Oh, we didn't do it all," said Midget. "Mrs. Adams and half a dozen other ladies have been working all the morning, too. And Mrs. Spencer sent a lot of lovely things. Why, the house is 'most full of furniture."

"I never heard of such a town," said Mrs. Mortimer, laughing. "I think, James, it would be a fine place to live."

"Yes," Mr. Mortimer agreed; "if you're sure to be burned out of house and home."

The village people did, indeed, prove themselves generous. In the afternoon the enthusiasm spread to such an extent, that curtains were being put to the windows, and kerosene poured into the lamps. Some of the more impetuous ones wanted to move the family in that night, but it was deemed better to wait until Monday. Marjorie was allowed to tell Mrs. Simpson what had been done for her.

"My gracious land!" exclaimed the poor woman. "I can't take it in, Miss Marjorie! A whole house! all furnished—for me? Oh, it's too much! You're too good! I don't deserve it."

"It's because we're so sorry for you, Mrs. Simpson," said Midget. "Mr. Simpson has been in the hospital so long, I wonder how you ever got along at all. But now, with this house for a start, you can manage, can't you?"

"Oh, yes, Miss Marjorie; I'm thinkin' Sam can get a job of some sort this spring. And I can do washin' now, for Hannah can mind the babies. Oh, Miss Marjorie, it's too good you are! You're just like your father and your dear mother."

And then, for the first time since the fire, Marjorie felt an absolutely clear conscience. She realized that she hadn't done wrong—at least, not intentionally; and though the circumstances had greatly annoyed Miss Larkin, and had disturbed one of her guests, yet now, the whole affair had turned out all right.

Indeed, the matter was practically taken out of Marjorie's hands; and though the Jinks Club did their full share of assisting, it was the grown-up citizens of Rockwell who escorted Mrs. Simpson and her children to their new home on Monday.

The house, though not lavishly, was completely furnished; the pantry was well stocked; so were the coal-bin and wood-box.

And though most of the Simpson children were too young to appreciate the kindness that had given them all this, poor, hard-working Mrs. Simpson showed gratitude true and deep enough to satisfy the most exacting.

"And while I humbly thank all you kind ladies," she said, her voice choked with emotion, "I can't forget that but for Marjorie Maynard, I'd have been in the poorhouse now!"

"Hooray for our Mopsy!" cried Flip Henderson, which turned into gay laughter what had threatened to be a tearful climax to the occasion.

CHAPTER XIII
A BIRTHDAY PLAN
"King," said Marjorie, suddenly, "I have the beautifullest idea in the world!"

"Spring it," said Kingdon, not looking particularly expectant. "Is it one of your crazy ones, or a really good one?"

"Oh, a really good one," declared Marjorie, whose enthusiasm was never dampened by King's preliminary lack of interest.

It was a rainy afternoon, and the children were amusing themselves in the living-room. Miss Larkin was up in her own room, writing letters, and the time really seemed ripe for an escapade of some sort.

"It's a big idea," went on Midget, "and you two must listen while I tell about it."

King and Kitty put both hands behind their ears, and leaned forward in exaggerated anxiety to hear the plan.

"Hope it's mischief," said King; "I've been good so long I'm just about ready to sprout wings. Let's cut up jinks."

"No," said Marjorie, severely; "it isn't mischief, and we're not going to cut up jinks. At least, not bad jinks. Not till Mother and Father come home, anyway. But I'm sort of hungry for a racket of some kind, myself. So let's do this. You know next week Wednesday is Miss Larkin's birthday."

"Yes, I know it," said Kitty; "how old is she?"

"Kit," said her brother, "I'm ashamed of you! You mustn't talk about grown-up people's ages. You ought to know that."

"Well, what's the sense of a birthday, if it doesn't mean how old you are?" demanded Kitty.

"Never mind that," resumed Marjorie; "we mustn't say a word about her age. I know that much myself. But, you see, we did upset her awf'ly when we bounced the Simpsons right into the middle of her grand dinner party, and I don't think she ever got over it."

"She's been nice about it, though," said King, thoughtfully.

"Yes, she has. Hasn't scolded us hardly a bit about it. And that's just why I think we might do something nice for her on her birthday, to sort of make up, you know."

"Hooray!" cried King. "That is a good idea, Mops. Let's have a regular celebration for her."

"And let's keep it secret," said Kitty. "A surprise is most of the fun of a birthday party."

"All right," agreed Midget. "Only I don't mean a party, you know. For a party, for her, we'd have to invite grown-ups—and we can't do that. I mean just a celebration in the afternoon to show her that we remember her birthday."

"And that we're sorry we spoiled her dinner party," added Kitty.

"Yep," said King. "Now, what sort of a celebration have you thought of, Mopsy?"

"Well, I haven't finished thinking yet, but I had a sort of idea of a parade."

"With drums and banners?" cried King, eagerly.

"Oh, I'll tell you," broke in Kitty, "we'll have floats!"

"Floats?" echoed the other two.

"Yes," declared Kitty, warming to her subject; "floats, like they had in the big parade in New York."

The magnitude of this idea nearly took away the breath of her hearers, but they rose to the occasion.

"Jiminy Crickets!" cried King, "you do beat all, Kit! 'Course we'll have floats—gay ones, you bet!"

Marjorie's eyes shone, as her imagination ran riot.

"We'll get all the Jinks Club in it," she said, "and we'll each have a float. How shall we make the floats, Kit?"

"Oh, easy enough," said that capable young person, with a toss of her head. "You just take an express wagon, or a doll's carriage, or anything on wheels———"

"A soap box?" broke in King.

"Yes, a soap box—anything you can drag, you know. And then you decorate it all up fancy, like the big floats were."

"Oh, Kitty!" cried Marjorie in rapture, "it will be perfectly elegant! Paper flowers and flags and bunting—oh!"

It was a grand scheme. Of course, it was all in honor of Miss Larkin's birthday, but incidentally the Jinksies bid fair to get their own fun out of it, too.

"We'll have a meeting of the Jinks Club to-morrow," said Marjorie, "and we'll have it over at Delight's, so Miss Larkin won't hear what we say. Do we all parade with these floats?"

"Yes," said Kitty, who was always director of a costume party. "We must all dress up, you know, and then drag our float behind us, or push it, if it's a doll's carriage."

"There are two express wagons down cellar," said King; "Rosy Posy's, and the one that used to be mine when I was a kid."

From the dignity of his fourteen years, King looked back at his toy express wagon with disdain. But viewed as a "float," it was a different matter.

"We'll have to decorate the floats somewhere else besides here," said Marjorie. "For if we set out to keep it secret from Miss Larkin, let's do it."

"All right; I guess Flip Henderson's father will let us work on 'em in their barn. They only use the garage now, and the barn is pretty much empty."

"Where'll we get the other three floats?" asked Marjorie. "Our two express wagons, and Rosy Posy's doll-carriage are all we have."

"Dorothy has a doll-carriage," said Kitty, "and Flip can find some sort of a rig."

"Oh, yes," said King. "We can fix up something, if it's only a box on wheels; and then you girls can decorate it."

"Shall we each make one float, or all make all of 'em?" asked Marjorie, who was thinking out details.

"Both," said Kitty, enigmatically; "I mean, we'll each plan out our own, and make it; and then, if we can help each other, we will."

"I don't know how the others will like it," observed King; "they'll be doing all this work for us, really."

"No, they won't," said Midget; "it's just a new sort of jinks, that's all. Then, of course, we'll all come in here, and have the celebration, and have a feast, and if they don't like that—I don't know why."

"Shall we give her presents?"

"Yes, of course. Little things, you know. I've only got about thirty-five cents left of my allowance."

"I've only ten," said Kitty, "but I'll make something for her—a pincushion, maybe."

"H'sh! here she comes!" whispered King, warningly, and the plans were dropped for the present, as Miss Larkin came into the room.

"Well, little busy ones," she said, "what are you doing now? Plotting some mischief?"

76

"No, Miss Larkin," said Midget. "Truly it's not mischief this time. Though King did say he was spoiling for some," she added, with a laughing glance at her brother.

"Yes, I did," he retorted; "and I think I'll have some! Girls, let's tease Larky!"

It was a strange thing, but the young Maynards always knew instinctively when Miss Larkin was in a mood to be teased, and would take it good-naturedly, or when she was in an austere mood, and would be angry if they trifled with her dignity.

But her indulgent smile at King's words was the signal for a general attack.

"All right; what shall we do with her?" cried Kitty.

"I'll tell you!" exclaimed Marjorie, and she ran across the hall to the drawing-room. "Come and help me, King," she called back.

And in a moment the two returned, lugging a tall, heavy cathedral candlestick, which was one of their mother's antique treasures.

It was of old brass, and was about six feet high. They stood this in the middle of the floor, and gravely announced that she was to be Joan of Arc, burnt at the stake.

"Here's the stake," said King, "and you're the ill-fated Joan. You must meet your fate bravely. Step up, Joan!"

Miss Larkin, giggling at their nonsense, stepped up, and stood against the candlestick. Meantime Kitty had procured lots of string, and with this they bound the helpless martyr to the stake.

"Miscreant!" began King, who loved to speechify.

"Oh, no," corrected Marjorie. "Joan of Arc wasn't a miscreant—she was a martyr."

"Well, martyr, then; Miss Martyr, I should say, we now bind thee to thy death pyre. Remember, oh remember, the misdeeds——"

"Oh, King," cried Kitty, "you're all wrong! I'll make the speech. Oh, fair martyr, who art thus brought low, forgive thy tyrants——"

"Who have struck the blow!" chimed in King. "I say, what was Joan burned up for, anyway? I ought to know, but I don't."

"Oh, read up your history afterward," cried Marjorie, impatiently. "Here, now we'll build the fire round her!"

With a dozen sofa-pillows, they built a very respectable fire, and by putting the red ones on tops anybody could imagine a blazing flame.

"Now, you must burn and shrivel up," commanded Kitty, and to their intense delight Miss Larkin entered quite into the spirit of the game.

"Burn me not up!" she cried; "I but did my duty!"

"Duty, forsooth!" shouted King. "You rode a white horse———"

"To Banbury Cross," supplemented Kitty, as her brother paused for breath.

At this, Joan of Arc giggled so hard, that she almost choked, and her humane captors loosed her bonds and set her free.

"You're a brick, Larky," said King; "why, even Mother can't play our romping games as good as you do. You'll have to have a reward!"

A tremendous wink at his sisters reminded them of the coming celebration, and they made warning faces at him, for King was apt to tell secrets unintentionally sometimes.

But after dinner, apparently for no reason at all, Miss Larkin's mood changed. She spoke in stern tones. She commanded the children to study their lessons quietly, and then go straight to bed.

"What's up?" said King to Marjorie, making no sound, but moving his lips.

"Dunno," she replied, in the same silent way, as they opened their schoolbooks.

Half an hour later, they filed quietly upstairs, and paused only for a moment's whispered conversation on the landing.

"Now, what do you s'pose ailed her?" asked King.

"I know," said Kitty, confidently; "she was sort of ashamed of having played Joan of Arc with us, and it made her more strict than ever."

"I guess that was it," said Marjorie, with a sigh. "But the celebration's off. I'm not going to make floats for an old crosspatch."

"Oh, pshaw!" said King. "You know how she is. She'll be sweet as pie on her birthday—you see if she isn't. And, anyway, we'll get as much fun out of the floats and things as she will."

This was true enough, so they said good-night, and separated.

"It's funny," said Marjorie to Kitty, after they reached their own room; "Mother and Father are always just the same,—even—you know. But Miss Larkin is awful indulgent one minute, and strict as anything the next."

"That's 'cause she isn't Mother and Father," said Kitty, wisely. "She's an old maid lady, you know, and she doesn't know how to treat children properly."

"You mustn't say 'old maid,' Kit; it isn't polite."

"I don't see why. But, I only mean, it takes a father or a mother to behave right to children. You know how ours are."

"Yes, I do," said Marjorie, in a contented voice. "They're just 'bout perfect. And I wish they'd come home."

"Well, it's no use wishing; they'll be gone more'n two weeks yet."

"Yes; so they will. And I guess we'll have the celebration, Kit; it'll fill up the time so."

"All right," said Kitty, sleepily, and then the two girls hopped into their two little white beds.

The next afternoon the Jinks Club met at Delight's. As they were planning the celebration, they behaved quietly, as, indeed, they were always expected to do at Mrs. Spencer's.

The Jinksies were quite ready to help with a birthday pageant for Miss Larkin.

They saw at once the possibilities of a lot of fun for themselves, and if, incidentally, it gave a grown-up lady pleasure, they had no objection, and, indeed, were rather glad.

"'Course we'll build the floats in our barn," said Flip Henderson. "It'll be gay. I'll use a wheelbarrow for mine. I know just how I'll fix it! You needn't laugh, either. Just wait till you see it!"

Though the idea of a wheelbarrow had made them laugh at first, they quickly realized its possibilities, and, too, Flip was an ingenious boy, and would doubtless fix it up beyond all recognition. Dorothy had a doll's carriage, which she said she would use; and Delight said she would borrow a neighbor's baby-carriage, as that would be just right for the float she already had in mind.

"Oh, won't it be lovely!" cried Marjorie, hugging Delight in her enthusiasm. "Shall we know about each other's floats or keep 'em secret?"

"Oh, let's know about 'em," said King; "it's more fun, and then we can help each other. I know I couldn't make one alone."

He looked helplessly at his sisters, and Marjorie said:

"'Course you couldn't. We'll make paper flowers and whatever you need. Now, let's decide on our floats. Shall we have 'em historical?"

"Oh, no!" cried Delight; "I thought you meant just pretty ones. Mine's going to be fairies."

"Lovely!" exclaimed Kitty. "I'll have mine mermaids. I saw a beautiful one in New York with mermaids."

"Huh!" said Flip, "you can't make mermaids, Kit; you're crazy. How would you do it?"

"I'll bet she can!" said King, whose faith in Kitty's inventive genius was unbounded.

"I know I can," said Kitty, calmly. "I'll just take some of Rosy Posy's dolls—her biggest ones—and then I'll make long taily things of green silk or something, and stuff 'em with sawdust, and stick the dolls' feet in, and sew 'em round the waist. Oh, it'll be as easy as pie!"

"I told you so," said King, looking proudly at his small sister. "Now, what shall I have, Kit?"

"Oh, you must think of your own subject, and then I'll help you rig it up."

"All right," said King; "my float will be sort of historical, after all. I'll have the discovery of the North Pole."

"Fine!" exclaimed Marjorie. "I'll help you, too! We'll make a whole Arctic region of cotton batting, like we had at the bazaar last winter!"

"I haven't decided on mine yet," said Flip, who was thinking hard. "The rest of you can choose first."

"We've all chosen, but Dorothy and me," said Midget; "and I know what mine'll be. What's yours, Dot?"

"I guess I'll just have flowers," said Dorothy, timidly. She was not so energetic as the others.

"Do," said Kitty; "you'll be sweet as a flower girl, and your float can be all flowers, with butterflies hovering over it, on sort of strings."

"Oh," cried Delight, with dancing eyes, "this will be a splendid show! We ought to let more people see it!"

"Say we do!" said Flip. "Let's parade all the way down Broad Avenue from our house to yours. Everybody will be glad to look at us!"

"I rather guess they will!" declared King. "All right, we'll do that, and we'll have Miss Larkin waiting for us on our verandah, and all march up in great style. Then, of course, you Jinksies will all come in to the celebration feast."

"I s'pose we'll have a Birthday Cake," suggested Kitty.

"That's going to be my float!" interrupted Marjorie. "I've just thought of it. A great, big cake, like a Jack Horner Pie, you know. And candles on it, and icing; and presents and things inside! Ellen will help me make it. I mean a great big one, as big as a barrel top. Then on an express wagon, or something like that, and decorated, it will be a float."

"Fine!" agreed King. "If Larky doesn't like her birthday this year, it won't be our fault, will it?"

After some more animated discussion of the wonderful project, the Jinksies had their usual light refection of cookies and lemonade, and then departed for their homes.

"Meet in Henderson's barn, at nine o'clock, to-morrow morning," said King, as they separated. "Bring your doll-carts, girls, and Delight, if you can't borrow Mrs. Phillips' baby-carriage, I'll fix you up a float. She may want it for her baby's use, you know."

"Well, I'll see, King. I think she'll let me have it, though."

The laughing crowd went across the street, and then separated again as the Maynards turned in at their own gateway.

CHAPTER XIV
HENDERSON PALACE

All day Saturday the members of the Jinks Club were busy making their "floats." Delight came in triumph, pushing a wicker baby-carriage ahead of her.

"Mrs. Phillips let me have it," she said, "because she says the baby uses the go-cart 'most all the time now, anyway."

In the carriage she had many rolls of tissue paper, and a big bundle of tarlatan, and gilt paper and wands, and all sorts of fascinating things. Delight loved to cut and paste, and long before the others began their work, she had flung off hat and coat, and was singing to herself as she made pink and white paper roses.

Kitty, too, was industrious, and she sat in a corner and sewed mermaids' tails diligently, but she was able to do her share of the talking as well.

"What's your float going to be, Flip?" she asked, not very clearly, by reason of some pins between her teeth.

"Now, don't you all laugh at me," began Flip, looking a little uncertain, "but as King says his float is historical, mine's going to be, too. Mine's the 'Declaration of Independence.' "

"Laugh!" exclaimed Kitty; "I should say we wouldn't! Why, that'll be grand, Flip. How are you going to do it?"

"Well; it's all done—that is, it's partly done. I haven't fixed up the wheelbarrow yet."

It was hard not to laugh at Flip—he was so earnest, and yet so humorous of face.

"Wait, I'll show you," he said; and then, from an adjoining room in the barn, he wheeled in a broad, old-fashioned wheelbarrow, on which sat a Roger's Group!

"That's it," he said, proudly. "I found that old bunch of statesmen up in the attic, and Mother said I could use it if I liked. Now, I say, when that dinky old wheelbarrow is all draped with a flag it'll look pretty fine, hey?"

"Gorgeous!" said Midget, with enthusiasm. "Your float is all right, Flip. You just wind those legs and handles and the wheel with red, white, and blue bunting, and there you are!"

"Well, I thought I'd paint the wheel. Blue rim with white stars on it, and red and white spokes, hey?"

"Yes, better plan," said King. "Stuff'll get all twisted in the wheel. Now, here's my express wagon, and here's my North Pole. Who'll help me build an Arctic Region?"

"I will," said Delight, dropping her paper flowers into the baby-carriage. "I can do mine afterward. Let me help you, King. I know just how."

"You're a brick, Flossy Flouncy!" exclaimed King, as he watched Delight's deft little fingers pile fleecy cotton batting round his North Pole in most realistic snowdrifts.

"I can't do anything on my float to-day," announced Kitty. "I have to get the mermaids done first, and they're such a bother."

"You make them too carefully," said Dorothy, as she watched Kitty patiently sewing spangles over the green fish-tails that were to transform Rosamond's dolls into mermaids.

"I don't care," said painstaking Kitty, "I like to have them nice. And Delight will help me fix the float, won't you?"

"'Course I will. We'll all help each other. Where's your float, Dorothy?"

"Well, I'm going to take Mother's old flower-stand, the kind with shelves, you know. She doesn't use it now, and she says I may have it. And I'm just going to set it on a flat platform with wheels; Flip says he'll make me one; and then just cram it all over with flowers. That's all."

"It will be lovely!" declared Delight; "there's nothing so pretty as flowers."

Under Miss Hart's wise tuition, and because she was truly trying to be less selfish, Delight was becoming a veritable little sunbeam. Everybody liked her, and as she tried to be sweet and helpful, she found it was not difficult, after all.

And now, in all this business of fancy fixings and decorations, Delight's nimble fingers and good taste were of great assistance.

Marjorie was working away at her "birthday cake." It was a large pasteboard bandbox, round, of course, and low. She was covering it with white crêpe paper, and making tiny festoons of the paper round the edge to look like fancy icing.

On top she pasted gilt letters, which read, "To Miss Larkin, from the Jinks Club." Inside were to be the presents, of course.

"But I don't want you other Jinksies to give presents to Miss Larkin," said Marjorie. "There's no reason why you should, you know. Just us Maynards will give the presents; and we're not going to give much."

"Oh, pooh," said Flip; "let us chip in, too; it won't hurt us to give some little thing. Mother'll get a handkerchief or something for me to give, I know."

"Yes, let us," said Delight. "In fact, my mother spoke of it herself. She said she'd get a little book for me to give."

"Of course, I'll give something, too," said Dorothy Adams. "I'd like to. And I think it would be nice if we gave things to each other, too. It would fill up the pie—cake, I mean."

"Ho!" said Flip; "'tisn't our birthdays, Dot."

"I don't care," said Dorothy, stoutly. She rarely made a suggestion, but when she did, she stood by it. "I mean just some little thing—a paper doll or a hair-ribbon."

"Well," said King, "I'd just love to have a paper doll; and as for a hair-ribbon, I need one awfully!"

Then they all laughed, but Dorothy would not be laughed down.

"Well," she said, "your few little presents for Miss Larkin will just rattle round in that great big pie."

"You're right, Dot," said Kitty, who generally saw matters very sensibly. "Let's give each other presents, only not everybody to everybody else. I mean, let's each give one present, and get one present."

"Oh, Kit, you mix me up so," groaned her brother. "Tell us more 'splicitly."

"All right," said Kitty, undisturbed, "here's what I mean. S'pose Mops gives to Delight, and Delight to King, and King to Dorothy, and Dorothy to me, and me—I, to Flip, and then Flip to Midget—that makes one apiece all round, doesn't it?"

"Katharine Maynard, you're a genius!" declared her brother; "you've set my head whizzing, but I grasp your idea. Now, let me see, who is it gives me a paper doll?"

"Delight does," returned Kitty, calmly; "and if you tease so, she will give you a paper doll, and it would serve you right, too!"

"Yes, it would," said King, so meekly, that they all laughed. "And on whom do I bestow a diamond necklace, or some such little trinket?"

"On me," said Dorothy, promptly; "Kitty said so."

"All right," said King, "your scheme, fair maidens, is a winner. Into the pie our gifts we'll throw—ha, ha, ha, and ho, ho, ho!"

"King, you're a lovely poet," said Marjorie, "but won't you come here now and help me fasten this pie on its wheels?"

"Certingly, certingly, my liege lady; hast any tackerinos?"

"No; but here's a hammerino. Can't you find some nails?"

"Ay, ay, in just a jiff!"

And sure enough, in a few moments Marjorie's big birthday cake sat proudly on a board across an express wagon, which, though a toy, was a good-sized affair.

"Now for the fiddle-de-dees!" cried King, as he picked up a pile of paper roses and strewed them on the cake.

"Oh, King, stop! You'll spoil it!" cried Marjorie, rescuing her treasures from her teasing brother. "But I wish you would help me put the candle-holders on."

They had plenty of candle-holders left from Christmas trees, and the next question was, how many they should put on the cake.

"Put 'em all on," said Flip, without hesitation.

"But there are seven dozen here in the box," said Marjorie; "that would look as if we thought she was eighty-four years old!"

"She isn't," said Kitty, seriously; "so that won't do."

Marjorie looked thoughtful.

"I don't think it's polite to put the number of her age on," she said, at last. "We don't know it, of course, but even if we guess at it, it wouldn't be polite."

"No," agreed Kitty, "you see, we might guess right."

"I suppose she's more'n twenty-one," observed Flip.

"Yes, she is," declared King. "She's older than my mother, I know that."

"Hush, King," said Midget; "you mustn't even talk about it. I guess we'll have to leave the candles off."

"Then it won't be a birthday cake at all," objected Delight.

"Well, I can't help it," said Marjorie, sighing; "it'll have to be a Jack Homer Pie, then. I can't be impolite to a lady on her own birthday!"

"I'll tell you what," said Kitty, slowly; and they all listened, for Kitty had a way of cutting Gordian knots for them. "You see, as we're all going to get presents, it's sort of our birthdays, too; not really, but just pretend. So let's add up all our ages—that'll make a lot, and then have that many candles. We can explain to Miss Larkin that we don't mean she's that old."

"Be sure to explain that to her, Kit," said her brother, gravely, after he had made a rapid calculation with the aid of his fingers and thumbs, "for it comes to about seventy!"

"Add in Rosy Posy," reminded Marjorie. "She can't be left out of a Maynard celebration."

"All right; call it seventy-five. Got that many candles, Mops?"

"Yes, more'n that."

"Well, put on seventy-five, and call it square."

"But the cake is round," said Delight, dimpling with fun.

"Oh, Flossy Flouncy, what a wit you are!" cried King. "All right, Mops, let's bang the seventy-five candle-holders into place, immejit. My, it's a lot, isn't it?"

But they were finally all in place, and Marjorie's float began to look really lovely. She had plenty of paper flowers to decorate with, and when the birthday came, she intended to wreathe the big cake with smilax, and festoon the sides of the float with the same pretty green.

"It isn't such a lot of work, after all," said Delight, as, when the noon whistle blew, the children put on their things to go home.

"Poor old Flossy Flouncy," said King; "how can you say so? You've been helping everybody else so much, your own wagon is scarcely touched."

"Oh, pooh!" said Delight, "I can finish that up this afternoon, or Monday afternoon, after school. What time is the parade, Marjorie?"

"Well, we want to start early, so as to have plenty of time for the celebration afterward. S'pose we say, leave the barn at three o'clock——"

"Oh, don't say barn!" exclaimed Delight; "it doesn't sound right. Say leave the——"

"Headquarters," suggested King. "No; that sounds like a fire brigade. Leave the Castle or the Palace, I'd say."

"All right," said Flip; "we've always called this place the barn, but we'd just as lieve change. Henderson Palace it is, at your service!"

"That's better," said Delight, smiling at him.

"Well, then," went on Marjorie, "we'll leave Henderson Palace at three o'clock next Wednesday, and, with our gorgeous floats, we'll parade down Broad Avenue to Maynard Castle—how's that?"

"All right," said Kitty; "then we'll storm Castle Maynard, and take the fair Lady Larkin captive."

"If she's in a good humor," put in King.

"She's bound to be, on her birthday," said Midge. "Well, then we'll make her and Rosy Posy queens of the feast, and then we'll all celebrate together."

"Sounds lovely!" said Dorothy. "And do we wear fancy dresses?"

"Sure!" said King. "Half the fun is in rigging up. We must each match our float, you know. I'll be an Arctic explorer."

"You can have Father's fur motor-coat," said Flip; "then you'll look the part first-rate."

"Good," said King; "and I know where I can catch a pair of snowshoes. What'll you be, Delight?"

"A fairy, of course. But can we go through the street in that sort of rigs?"

"Oh, yes," said Marjorie; "just down Broad Avenue. Everybody knows us. And, anyway, it's just like the pageant in New York; they went on the streets in fancy clothes."

"It's more like the Baby Parade in Asbury Park," said Dorothy; "I saw that once, and the children wore all sorts of pretty costumes. And they had baby-carriages, decked out with every sort of thing."

"All right, then," said Midget, who was vigorously pulling on her gloves; "I guess I'll fix up my fancy dress this afternoon, and finish up these float things Monday and Tuesday. We've time enough, anyway."

"Yes," said Delight, "that's what I said. It doesn't take long to make floats." She tucked her arm through Marjorie's, and the two skipped away, followed by Dorothy and Kitty.

"What have you children been doing all the morning?" asked Miss Larkin, as they were all seated at the lunch-table.

"Playing in Mr. Henderson's barn," said Marjorie, promptly.

This was well enough, but Miss Larkin, who was in high good humor, seemed possessed to ask questions.

"What did you play?" she said.

She really had no curiosity on the subject, she asked merely with a desire to appear interested in their interests, but it did seem a pity she should be so insistent to-day of all days.

"Oh, we played——" began Marjorie, and then she stopped. She had no inclination to be other than truthful, but the truth she did not want to tell.

"Well, we played——" supplemented King, with a desire to help Marjorie out of her quandary, but he, too, came to a standstill.

"Well, well!" said Miss Larkin, shaking a playful finger at the red-faced trio, "you must have been up to something naughty, if you can't tell me about it. Oh, fie, fie, little Maynards!"

When Miss Larkin took this tone, she was particularly aggravating, and it was Kitty who threw herself into the breach, and saved the day by her ready wit.

"Larky, dear," she began, and Miss Larkin smiled gaily at the nickname, "we truly weren't up to any mischief, but we beg you as a special favor not to ask us what we were doing— because—well, because it's a sort of a secret."

"A secret, bless your hearts! Then, of course, I don't want to know. All children love secrets. Keep yours, my dearies; I didn't mean to be curious, I assure you."

Now here was a nice spirit, indeed! Such a Larky was well worth making a celebration for, and the children's spirits rose accordingly.

After luncheon, Ellen had to be interviewed.

With great secrecy, and much careful closing of doors, Marjorie and Kitty held a whispered consultation with the good-natured cook.

Ellen consented to all their requests. She agreed to make a birthday cake of real flour and eggs, besides the "float" cake, and she seemed more than willing to prepare a feast that would be acceptable to a hungry Jinks Club, as well as to the heroine of the occasion.

All was to be kept secret from Miss Larkin, so that the celebration might be a complete surprise.

"Ice cream, of course," whispered Kitty.

"Sure, Miss Kitty," said Ellen. "Wud ye like it pink an' white, now; or wid a bit o' choc'lit?"

"Just pink and white," said Kitty, after a moment's consideration; "and then choc'late on the cakes, Ellen. Little cakes, you know; all different colors."

"Lave all to me, Miss Kitty; sure I'll fix the table so grand as ye niver saw it afore. It's likin' Miss Larkin, I do be; though I'll not deny she's a bit quare at times. But she's a kind lady, an' I'm glad she's goin' to have a party."

"Now, we must think up our presents," said Midget, as the two girls went up to their own room. "What shall we give Miss Larkin?"

"Well, I'll make her a pincushion, as I said. I can make a lovely one out of pink with lace over it, and little bows."

"Yes, you're good at those things, Kit. I can't sew very well; I guess I'll get her a bottle of violet water. Mother always thinks that's a nice present. And then we must see about presents for each other, you know. I'm to give to Delight, so that's easy. She likes everything. I guess I'll take one of those lovely views Mother sent last, and frame it in passe-partout; she can hang it on her bedroom wall."

"That'll be lovely," said Kitty. "You make those frames so neatly, Mops. But I have to think of something for Flip; that's awful hard."

"Oh, no, 'tisn't; make some of that cocoanut fudge—the new recipe; and then fill a pretty box, and tie it up with a ribbon. He'll love it."

"That is a good idea; I believe I'll do that. I won't make it until Wednesday morning; I can do it before school, and then it'll be fresh."

"Yes," agreed Midget, "and while you're about it, Kit, make enough, so we can have some, too."

CHAPTER XV
A FINE CELEBRATION
April had only used up about a week of her showers and sunshine, and the Jinks Club feared she might send a few of her mischievous raindrops on their parade, but when the birthday came at last, the weather was quite as smiling as the faces of the six paraders.

The floats were finished, and though some were the least bit wobbly, their owners fondly hoped they would last through the line of march. Miss Hart had agreed to go over to call on Miss Larkin that afternoon, in order to insure the presence of the Birthday Lady at the right time.

Nurse Nannie promised to have Rosy Posy in gala attire, and ready to take her part in the festivities.

The fancy costumes had been taken over to Flip's house, and Mrs. Henderson was quite willing to assist the little masqueraders in their toilettes.

Indeed, she said the children looked so pretty, it was too bad they were not going to be on exhibition at some bazaar or entertainment. Just at three o'clock the parade started.

Kingdon went first. He was a tall boy for his years, and so Mr. Henderson's fur motor-coat just escaped touching the ground. The April sunshine was a bit warmish, but King valiantly encased himself in his furs, cap, earflaps, and all, and rather awkwardly stumbling along on his snowshoes, dragged his float behind him.

The float itself was beautiful. With Delight's help, King had arranged an Arctic Region of cotton snowdrifts, from the centre of which rose a most imposing North Pole. This was white, also, and glistening with the tinsel frost that is used for Christmas trees. To its top was nailed the Stars and Stripes, and the flag fluttered proudly as the float wobbled along. A crowning glory was seen in good-sized lumps of real ice that nestled among the white drifts. And over these realistic glaciers clambered white "Teddy Bears," of which Rosy Posy's "Boffin" was perhaps the finest specimen. Also, an Eskimo doll, borrowed from the Maynard nursery, added local color to the scene.

The float would have done credit to a grown-up, and King pulled it proudly along, though hampered by his rather unmanageable snowshoes and cumbersome coat.

"Old King Cole, discovered the Pole," chanted Delight, as King started down the Hendersons' driveway, and then they all took up the refrain and repeated it with enthusiasm.

The second float was Delight's. Fairies, of course, as they were her specialty. She was dressed as a fairy herself, and on her lovely golden hair rested a gilt paper crown, with tall points. A long gilt wand, with a star on the end, was her sceptre, and her frock of white tarlatan was made with many frills, and spangled with gilt stars. Two gauzy wings fluttered from her shoulders, and her white slippers showed a tiny gilt star on each.

"Oh, Delight," cried Marjorie. "You do look too perfectly lovely for anything! Doesn't she, Mrs. Henderson?"

"Yes, indeed," returned that lady, smiling; "but you all look so lovely, it's hard to choose among you."

Delight pushed her float, instead of drawing it, for it was the wicker baby-carriage that she had borrowed; but so transformed, that not a speck of wicker could be seen. It was twined and draped with green and white tarlatan; from its wicker hood, or top, depended filmy curtains, which were tied back to afford a view of the fairy scene inside. Here, in a sort of little bower, were dolls dressed as fairies, dancing round in a magic ring.

But, dainty as they were, no doll was so sweet as Delight, herself, with her golden hair flying, and her pretty face smiling at the fun of it all.

Fairy bells hung round the edges of the float, and jingled as it rolled along.

Delight stepped slowly, lest she run into the North Pole, whose brave explorer floundered on, guiding his snowshoes as best he might.

Then, after the Fairy Float, came Dorothy, the Flower Girl.

Her mother had fixed up a charming costume from one of Dorothy's own pretty little frocks, by sewing tiny artificial roses all over it. A wreath of flowers on her head made her look almost like a May Queen.

Her float, though not so ingenious as some, was quite as pretty as any.

The old-fashioned flower-stand, of green wire, was filled with growing spring flowers in pots, and the pots were concealed by smilax and asparagus fern. The body and wheels of the float were covered entirely with pink and white paper roses, and the whole effect was of a mass of blossoms.

Then came Kitty with her Mermaids. This float was the most ambitious of all, and though a success, it was liable to drop to pieces at any minute. Kitty had tried to represent the billowy ocean, and her waves were of dark-green cambric, with wires underneath to make the billows wave. On this uncertain sea were perched several mermaids. These were highly successful as works of art, for the spangled green tails, stuffed with sawdust, looked just like those shown in pictures, and the flaxen hair of the wax dolls' heads was truly mermaidish.

Kitty, herself, proudly represented Undine. Some green tarlatan was draped over her white frock, and paper seaweed hung all over her. A wreath of artificial water-lilies was extremely becoming, and her long hair hung in a curly mass.

Altogether, Kitty's float was wonderful, and she was optimistic enough to feel sure it would reach home in safety.

"Drive up near the North Pole, Kit," sang out Flip; "then that jiggly green ocean of yours will freeze, and there'll be no danger of its spilling over."

"'Twon't spill," said Kitty, serenely, and Undine trundled her ocean along happily, while the mermaids swayed about, and would have fallen off, but that their tails were securely fastened to the wires.

After Kitty, came Marjorie. Her float was the Birthday Cake, and a fine show it made.

Like Dorothy's, the float itself was covered closely with pink and white roses, for it was so easy to make paper roses, that they could have them by hundreds. And there is nothing prettier for fanciful decoration.

High up on a rose-covered soap-box sat the cake; white, and gilt-lettered, and wreathed about with fresh smilax. On it were the seventy-five candles, not lighted yet, and inside it nestled all the presents, tied in tissue paper and ribbons.

Midget, herself, wore a fancy costume she had once worn at a masquerade party.

It was a "Folly" dress, and was in blue and white stripes, with little bells on the pointed edges. There was a Folly cap with bells on, and the gay little garb was most becoming to merry Midget.

Last of all came Flip. His wheelbarrow was stunning in its red, white and blue draperies, and the Plaster Group of noble signers stood firmly in place as he trundled the vehicle along. Flip wore a Continental suit, and was supposed to represent George Washington, but as his white cotton-wool wig proved rather warm, and he was not so patient as King, he carried the wig and cocked hat under his arm, until he should reach the party.

And so, his round, freckled face, and somewhat obstreperous hair, surmounting the brass-buttoned blue coat, rather spoiled the illusion of the Father of our Country.

"Hey, you!" called out King, from the other end of the parade, "put on your head-rigging. You spoil the show!"

"Can't help it," Flip called back. "It's too roasting hot! I'll put it on when we get there."

"Hot! pooh!" shouted King, in scorn. "What d'you think of me! I'm melting in this fur envelope, but I keep it on just the same!"

"All right, keep it on," returned Flip, amicably, and the incident was closed.

Slowly, and thoroughly enjoying themselves, the parade moved down Broad Avenue.

People flew to the windows to watch them, or stepped out on their verandahs to see them go by. They received great applause, and many enthusiastic spectators begged them to stop a moment, or came out and walked by their side to examine the curious floats. At last, they turned into the Maynards' place.

Flip hastily clapped on his wig and hat, and the parade marched up the drive.

"Ought to have had music!" exclaimed King. "Never thought of it till this minute!"

"Sing," suggested Delight.

"All right; start her up."

But asked so suddenly, Delight couldn't think of anything appropriate. In a frantic attempt, however, to supply the desired music, she began "John Brown's Body."

Everybody joined in, lustily, and as the front door opened, and Miss Hart gently pushed the bewildered Miss Larkin forward, a rousing "Glory, glory, Hallelujah!" greeted her.

"What—what is it all?" cried the amazed lady, as right in front of her was a strange-looking figure much like a clumsy bear, trying to make a dancing-school bow, or rather, a dancing-bear bow, without tumbling over his snowshoes.

"Go on, King!" shouted Marjorie. "March round."

So King went on, and the parade slowly went round the big oval of the Maynard front lawn two or three times.

Miss Larkin was fairly enraptured.

"For me! for my birthday!" she exclaimed, as Miss Hart explained it to her. "Why, I never saw anything so wonderful! Go round again, children, dear! Oh, you are fine!"

She clasped her hands in ecstasy, and Rosy Posy fairly screamed in delight.

At last, they lined up the floats in front of the verandah, and then the six, joining hands, repeated the birthday poem, which King had made up for the occasion. Kitty thought it wasn't very poetical, but she had been too busy with her mermaids to make a poem herself, so they had all learned King's. They didn't sing it, but they recited it in such a sing-song voice, that it was just as good.

"Larky, Larky!

Harky, Harky!

To our Birthday ode.

While we sing

As we bring

Presents, quite a load!"

It wasn't very poetical, perhaps, but the enthusiasm of its recital so pleased Miss Larkin, that she wanted to have it repeated several times, and her request was obligingly granted.

"Now," said Marjorie, "shall we have the presentation of gifts first, or the feast?"

"Gifts," said practical Kitty; "then the supper, and then it will be time for the party to be over. If it isn't, we can play games."

"You see," said Midget, who had sidled up to Miss Larkin, "we thought we disturbed your dinner party, when Mrs. Mortimer was here, so this is sort of to make up, you know."

"You dear child!" exclaimed Miss Larkin. "You didn't need to 'make up,' but this is the most wonderful birthday party I ever saw, and I can't tell you how I appreciate it."

"It's a celebration," explained Marjorie. "There are floats, you know, and altogether it's a pageant, like they have in New York. Isn't it grand! And the float that I dragged is your birthday cake. We're going to take it in the house to open it."

"And we don't think you're seventy-five years old," broke in Kitty. "We know you're not. But the candles stand for our ages, because we don't want to be impolite to you."

"Yes, that's all right," said Miss Hart, heading off any further allusions to the age of the lady who was receiving all this honor. "Now, let's get the cake into the house. Where shall we put it?"

"Well," said Midget, considering, "if we have the presents first, let's open the cake before we go into the dining-room. So let's take it into the living-room."

"Right, oh!" exclaimed King, and he and Flip carried the big cake indoors and they all followed.

Marjorie and Kitty, as chief hostesses, each took Miss Larkin's arm, and escorted her to a seat of honor.

"Now, Larky, Larky—harky, harky!" said King, with a flourish. "We hereby present you with this beautiful birthday cake, from your loving friends of the Jinks Club."

King had discarded his fur coat and snowshoes, but he had grabbed a few garlands of paper flowers from Dorothy's float, so that he would still look in festive array.

"I am overcome," said Miss Larkin, who seemed really bewildered at this further compliment offered her.

"Of course you are!" rejoined King. "We expected you to be. We'd have been much disappointed if you hadn't been overcome. Now, that's all right, so please recover your equilibrium, and we'll proceed to see what happens 'when the pie was opened.'"

"Very well," smiled Miss Larkin; "go ahead. I can stand it now."

Then King and Flip lifted off the cover of the big box, and left exposed the great pile of dainty parcels. Everybody had a gift, and, of course, Miss Larkin had a great many.

Though not of great value, they were all dainty and pretty little souvenirs, and Miss Larkin had real tears in her eyes, as she received one after another.

"It's like Christmas!" exclaimed Flip, as he smiled with pleasure at the box of fudge given him by Kitty.

"Don't open it now," warned King; "take it home with you; 'cause we're going to the dining-room in a minute."

"All right," said Flip, "but it looks greedy not to pass it around."

"No, it doesn't," said Kitty; "'cause it's your present. It only just happens to be a pass arounder. If it was a paper doll or a hair ribbon, you couldn't pass it around. So—you see."

"I see," agreed Flip, laying the box aside, but he did feel a little embarrassed about it.

However, just then Sarah threw open the dining-room doors, and they all marched out. King offered his arm to Miss Larkin, and Flip followed, escorting Miss Hart, who, though not taking an active part, was of great assistance in her pleasant, unostentatious way. The girls followed, and Rosy Posy toddled along with them.

Ellen and Sarah had really outdone themselves in arranging an attractive feast. No one had helped them, but the experienced servants knew well just what to do.

In the centre of the table was a large, round birthday cake, which could really be eaten. It was covered with white frosting, and in pink frosting were the initials of Miss Larkin's name, and the date of the day, with no reference to the year.

Dainty sandwiches were served first, with lemonade or milk, as the children chose.

Then there were little fancy cakes, and ice cream, and lovely jelly, and bon-bons, and nuts, and fruit, and every sort of delicacy that Ellen considered appropriate.

And then, as a final ceremony, the birthday cake was cut. Miss Larkin cut it herself, as was appropriate, and as she plunged the knife into the rich plum cake, she declared she was inspired to make a speech.

"Speech! Speech!" cried King, and they all clapped their hands and cheered.

"Dear children," began Miss Larkin, "I think you are the dearest and best children I ever knew. I think it was sweet of you to do all this for me on my birthday, and I shall never forget it."

That was all of the speech, and if it was simple and short, it was also most sincere and heartfelt.

The children were quiet for a moment—the earnest voice had made them a little serious—and then Flip said, "Three cheers for Miss Larkin!" and they gave them with a will.

As the noise subsided, Miss Larkin smiled and said:

"Three cheers for the Jinks Club!"

The club saw nothing incongruous in cheering themselves, so this cheer was as loud as the first.

Then, the hours had slipped away so fast, it was really time to go home, so the Jinks Club adjourned, after hearty good wishes and good-byes.

Thomas and James agreed to drag the floats back to Mr. Henderson's barn, to stay there until the Jinksies could attend to them.

So, after the guests had gone, the jolly crowd in the Maynard home spent an enthusiastic hour in discussing every bit of the celebration all over again, and congratulating themselves on its splendid success.

CHAPTER XVI
WINDOW BOXES

"It just seems to me," said Marjorie, at breakfast one morning, "that I must go out and dig."

"Dig for what?" asked King; "buried treasure?"

"No, not dig for anything, except just to dig. It's so springish outdoors, and so—well, such diggy weather."

"Oh! You mean to plant things," said King. "Well, let's all make gardens. It's Saturday, and we can dig 'em this morning, and plant 'em this afternoon, and there you are!"

"Yes," said Kitty, scornfully, "there you are! Who's going to water them all summer, and weed them? You know very well, Mops, that when we didn't keep our gardens nice last spring, Father said we couldn't have any this year."

"I know it; that's what's bothering me. I know we can't have gardens, but I do want to dig."

93

"Oh, well," said King, "go and dig in the sand-heap. That won't do any harm, and you can dig as long as you like."

"No," said Midget, disconsolately; "I want to plant a garden. I wish Father hadn't said we couldn't. If he was here, I'm sure I could coax him to let me do it. I'd keep it weeded and watered this year—I know I would."

"Yes; if Thomas did it all for you," laughed King. "No, Mopsy Midget, you're too careless to take care of a garden. Take your big brother's advice, and don't begin on schemes that you can't carry out."

"But I want to dig," said Marjorie, again.

"Mopsy Maynard," said King, "I've got that thoroughly in my head. I'm positively convinced that you want to dig, but I've done all I can in the matter, so don't repeat that information for my benefit."

"I want to dig," said Marjorie, in just the same tone; saying it, now, of course, merely to tease her brother.

"I dig wiv oo, Middy; we dig togevver," volunteered Rosy Posy, always willing to do anything for her adored Midget.

"All right, Rosy Posy. You and I'll go dig down deep in the ground, and p'raps we'll find something nice."

"Ess," said the baby, with an affirmative nod of her curly head; "ess, we find nice woims."

This made them all laugh, except Miss Larkin, who gave a little shudder at Rosy Posy's suggestion.

"Marjorie," she said, after a moment, "I've an idea for your digging, if you really want to dig."

"Well, I do feel like it, Miss Larkin, but I was mostly fooling. For Father did tell us we couldn't have gardens this year, and I was glad of it when he said it, but now I've just taken a notion to dig."

"It's the spring," said Kitty, sagely. "Spring always makes you feel diggy. But you'll get over it, Mops."

Kitty's philosophical remarks, though not always comforting, were usually founded on fact.

"But, children, listen," said Miss Larkin, who sometimes had difficulty to get an opportunity to speak. "This is my idea. You know your mother and father will be home week after next."

"Hooray! Hooray!" shouted King. "'Scuse me, Miss Larkin, but I sure am glad!"

"Me too—me too—me too," chanted Marjorie, until Kitty cried out:

"I'm glad, myself, but Mops, do stop singing a dirge about it."

"What is a dirge, Kit?" asked King. "You do use such awfully grown-up words. You oughtn't to do it at nine years old. What'll you be when you're as old as I am?"

"I hope I'll be less noisy than you two are," said Kitty, but she smiled good-naturedly at her more boisterous brother and sister. "Anyway, I think we all might be quiet long enough to let Miss Larkin say what she wants to."

"I think so, too," said Midget. "Go ahead, Larky, dear. Tell us about this digging scheme of yours."

"Well," began Miss Larkin, almost timidly, for when the children grew noisy, it always made her nervous, "it seemed to me it would be nice to prepare a little surprise for your parents' homecoming."

"Oh!" groaned King; "no more pageants for me! No more floats or celebrations or North Poles at present! No more marching half a mile wrapped in buffalo robes! Nay, nay, Pauline."

"Oh, King, do be still," begged Kitty. "Go on, Miss Larkin."

"And I thought, children dear, that it would be nice to get some window boxes and piazza boxes, and plant bright flowers in them. Then, you see, Marjorie, you can dig and plant, and yet not disobey your father's command not to make a garden. For, of course, he meant a garden on the ground, didn't he?"

"Yes, he did," said Midget. "I think window boxes would be fine! Tell us more about it, Larky, dear."

Pleased at the interest they all showed, Miss Larkin went on:

"I've arranged a great many myself, so I know just how. And it's very pretty work, and though, of course, it's some trouble, it's not nearly so much as a garden."

"It's beautiful!" cried Marjorie; "I'm crazy to get at it. Can we begin now? Aren't you through your breakfast, Miss Larkin? You don't want any more coffee, do you? Come on, let's get to work!"

"Oh, Marjorie, you'll drive me distracted!" cried the poor lady, clapping her hands to her head. "I 'most wish I hadn't proposed it."

"Please excuse her, Miss Larkin," said King. "She's a bad-mannered young thing, but I'll tame her."

Jumping up, King caught off Marjorie's hair-ribbon and ran round the table with it. Of course, Midget ran after him, and a general scramble followed.

Watching her chance to get out of the room without tumbling over the combatants, Miss Larkin escaped, and, running up to her own room, locked herself in.

"Now, you've made her mad, King," said Marjorie, reproachfully. She wasn't a bit annoyed, herself, at King's capers, but it was quite evident that Miss Larkin was.

"What geese you two are," remarked Kitty. "I don't see why you want to carry on so."

95

"Look out, Kit, or you'll lose your own hair-ribbon," said King, grinning, as he made a threatening move toward her big blue bow.

"Oh, take it if you want it," said Kitty, pulling it off, herself, and offering it politely to her brother.

Of course, this made them all laugh, and as Marjorie tied Kitty's ribbon again in place, and Kitty tied hers, they debated what they should do.

"Let's write a note and say we're sorry, and stick it under her door," said Midget.

This seemed a good plan, and they all agreed.

"You write it, King," said Kitty. "'Cause you write the best of all of us."

So King wrote, and they all suggested subject-matter for the effusion.

"Dear Miss Larkin:" the note began.

"Shall I say we're sorry?" asked King.

"Oh, that sounds so silly," objected Marjorie; "I mean so—so sensible, you know. Let's say something to make her laugh."

"Say this," suggested Kitty: "Three miserable sinners crouched outside your door, await your pardon."

"That's fine," said King, approvingly; "go on, Kit."

"We do want to dig," put in Marjorie, "and we want to make window boxes, and we want to make them quick."

"That goes," said King, writing rapidly; "next?"

"We're still crouching," went on Kitty, "we really will be, you know—and we hope you'll open the door right away, and say bless you, my children. And then we'll fly on the wings of the wind to do your bidding."

"A little highfalutin," commented King, "but I guess it'll do."

They all signed the document, and then raced upstairs. Poking it under Miss Larkin's door, they all crouched and waited.

Soon her voice came to them, through the keyhole.

"Are you all crouching there?" she said.

"Yes!" was the reply in concert.

"Well, I'll forgive you, if you'll promise not to tumble around so, and pull off hair-ribbons. It isn't pretty manners, at all."

96

"That's so, Miss Larkin," said honest King; "and I'm awful sorry. Come out—shed the light of your blue eyes upon us once more, and all will be forgiven."

Laughing in spite of herself, Miss Larkin opened the door, and found the three children crouching on the floor, their faces buried in their hands. As the door opened, they gave a long, low, wailing groan, previously agreed upon, and then they jumped up, smiling.

"Dear Miss Larkin," said King, with overdone politeness, "may we invite you to go window-boxing with us? It's a delightful day, and we want——"

"We want to dig," interrupted Marjorie.

"Yes, we'll set about it at once," said Miss Larkin, briskly.

It had suddenly occurred to her that the best way to quiet these turbulent young people was to get them occupied.

"My intention is," she said, "to present you children with the window boxes, and the plants. Then, after we set them out, of course, you will have to take care of them—or Thomas will. But I'm sure you'll enjoy doing it yourself, and, as I said, they will make a lovely greeting for your parents on their return."

"Where do we get the boxes?" King burst out, rather explosively, for he was trying to repress his over-enthusiasm.

"I think we can get them all ready made, at Mr. Pettingill's shop. I saw some there the other day. That's what made me think of it. Get your hats, and we'll go and see."

At last, here was a start. They flew for their hats, the girls taking the precaution to hang on to their hair-ribbons, for King was in mischievous mood this morning.

In less than ten minutes they started, King and Miss Larkin walking decorously ahead, and the two girls walking demurely behind.

At the shop, they found boxes already painted green, and built in the most approved fashion as to lining of zinc and pipe drainage.

They selected three, two to be placed on either side of the front verandah, and the other across Mrs. Maynard's bedroom window, which was in the middle of the house, in the second story.

These were bought and ordered sent home, and the shopkeeper promised to send them at once.

So the quartette went next to the florist's.

Here they grew quieter, for they became greatly interested in listening to Mr. Gilbert's advice about plants for boxes.

After careful consideration of the various flowers, they made their choice.

Each was expected to select plants for one box, and then to plant and care for that especial box all summer.

Marjorie was given the box for her mother's window; and she chose scarlet geraniums, with ferns for a background, and a border of sweet alyssum in front.

"You may have some trouble with them 'ere ferns, Miss," said the good-natured florist. "But if you do, an' if 'tain't your fault, you come back here, and I'll give you new ones fer 'em. That maidenhair fern's pretty hard to raise."

"Oh, I'll be very careful," said Marjorie, confidently. "I think it will grow all right."

"Everybody allus thinks that," said Mr. Gilbert, with a twinkle in his eye. "But if by any chance it don't, you come an' tell me ter wonst."

Kitty and King had the other two boxes, and, of course, had to select plants that harmonized with each other. Kitty chose French dwarf petunias, whose ruffled flowers excited her admiration as soon as she saw them. The colors were various shades of rose pink, and also white ones.

Then a trailing vine, known as Vinca Major, was selected to hang down and cover the front of the box, "like a frizzly bang," Kitty said.

King's flowers were verbenas, of the same colors as Kitty's blossoms, and he, too, had the green vine for a fringe. They bought, too, some mignonette to form a background, and then Miss Larkin said they had enough plants.

The florist's boy started at once with their purchases, and by the time they had walked home, all the things were ready for them to begin.

Thomas was called upon to help, and he worked under Miss Larkin's directions; but all such portions of the work as the children could do, were done by their little hands.

In the bottom of the boxes they had to put a layer of small stones. This was fun, for the stones had to be picked up from the driveway, and great care was used in getting good shapes and sizes.

Then some charcoal was sprinkled in, and after that the dirt was put in.

Thomas provided them with the right sort of soil, and at last Marjorie was able to dig to her heart's content.

"Isn't it fun!" she exclaimed, as, with hat and coat tossed off on the grass, she dug with a trowel, and also with her ten grimy little fingers. James and Thomas had set the boxes in their places, and fastened them firmly, and when it was time to put in the flowers themselves, Midget fairly jumped for joy.

To plant her box, she had to get out of another window onto the roof, but as Thomas took care she didn't roll off in her enthusiasm, she was safe while at work.

First she put in the ferns at the back; Miss Larkin advising from her standpoint inside Mrs. Maynard's room, and Thomas and Marjorie doing the actual planting. Then the lovely scarlet geraniums, and in front of them the tiny plants of sweet alyssum. This wasn't yet in bloom, but they hoped it would be by the day of Mrs. Maynard's arrival.

Also, Miss Larkin and Thomas helped the other two young gardeners below stairs.

King's and Kitty's boxes were longer than Marjorie's, as they were verandah boxes.

King grew a little impatient at the necessary slowness of the work, and willingly accepted Thomas's help; but Kitty was ambitious to do it all herself, and worked away untiringly.

It took nearly the whole day, but at last, when four o'clock found the boxes all complete, and a lovely mass of bright blossoms, the Maynards, though too tired for vigorous romping, were exuberant with joy.

"It was the loveliest idea, Larky!" said Marjorie, patting the lady's face, with hands that showed traces of good brown earth. "I'm so glad you thought of it."

"So'm I," said Kitty and King, together.

"Now, go and get tidied," said Miss Larkin, "and then I'll give you further instructions."

This didn't sound very interesting, but when they came back to the living-room an hour later, clean, and rested, they found Miss Larkin waiting for them, with most attractive-looking little books in her hands.

They proved to be little notebooks, in which she had written just what they must do through the coming months, to keep their plants in good order. Every direction was clearly given; every contingency was provided for; and Kitty said:

"Well, if those posies don't grow right, it will be our fault, not theirs."

"It won't be my fault," said Midget, with determination. "I'm going to take care of my flowers awful carefully. 'Cause I want to show Father that I've improved since last year."

"That's the right spirit," said Miss Larkin, approvingly; "try to do better each year, and thus grow up to be good and worthy women."

"I can't do that," said King, with a sigh, "but probably I'll grow up to be President."

CHAPTER XVII
DELIGHTFUL ANTICIPATIONS
"Won't it be fun!" exclaimed Marjorie, as, with King and Kitty and Delight, she came into the house; "let's sit down and talk it all over again."

"What's it all about?" asked Miss Larkin, smiling at the happy faces of the four.

"Well, it's going to be Arbor Day next week, and the ladies of the church are going to have a festival," explained Midget; "and they want you to help—Miss Merington is coming to see you about it—and they've asked us children to help."

"Why, what can you do at a grown-up festival?"

"Oh, we can do lots," said Kitty; "we sell things, you know, and—and just help round."

"Yes," put in King, "and we give 'em things to sell, too. Make 'em or buy 'em or something."

"Or get them given to us," suggested Delight. "The shopkeepers are awfully generous about that."

"What kind of a festival is it?" asked Miss Larkin.

"Oh, that's the fun of it," said Marjorie. "It's an Arbor Day affair, you know, and they call it the Arbor Show, and it's all trees."

"All trees?"

"Yes; the big hall is all to be filled with trees—not real trees—but sort of made-up ones, and then we sell things off of them."

"Oh, I begin to see. The trees are instead of the usual booths."

"Yes, that's it. Each lady has a tree, and then she gets her friends, or children, or anybody to help her. Miss Merington asked Delight and me to be with her. She has the Orange Tree."

"Oh; and do you sell oranges?"

"Yes, real oranges, and other kinds, too."

"And do they want me to have a tree? What kind shall I choose? And will you children be with me?"

Miss Larkin was greatly interested in the project, for not often did she get an opportunity to take part in such an entertainment.

"You'll have to see what Miss Merington says," said Marjorie. "She's at the head of it all, and she said she'd come to see you this afternoon."

"Oh, did she? Then I'll run and change my gown; I'd rather look more dressy when she comes."

Miss Larkin bustled away, and King said:

"I'll like to have a tree with Larky. She'll buy a lot of things for us, and she'll be so 'thusiastic about it. Hey, Kit?"

"Yes," agreed Kitty, "and I'd rather be with her, than a stranger lady, anyway."

Soon Miss Merington came to call, and Miss Larkin came down to meet her, resplendent in a silk costume and her best jewelry.

Miss Merington was a charming young woman, and though only slightly acquainted with Miss Larkin, she laid the case before her so prettily, that Miss Larkin gladly consented to assist at the bazaar.

"You see," explained Miss Merington, "as it's an Arbor Day, we have trees instead of tables or booths. For instance, there will be a nut tree, and under that the attendants will sell all sorts of good things made with nuts; nut cake, nut candy, salted nuts, glacé nuts, and everything they can think of. And, too, they'll have those funny little dolls made of peanuts, and those grotesque heads made of cocoanuts. Oh, there are lots of lovely things for the Nut Tree."

"Doughnuts," suggested Miss Larkin.

"Why, yes, of course," said Miss Merington, laughing. "They're fine nuts to sell from a nut tree."

"What other trees will there be?" asked Marjorie, who sat looking admiringly at the visitor. She greatly admired Miss Merington, and, also, that young lady had a warm affection for Marjorie. She had asked the two girls to assist her at her own tree, knowing they would be glad to be together, and that they were capable enough to be really helpful to her in her work.

"Well, there's the Dogwood Tree," said Miss Merington. "They will sell any thing that has to do with dogs. They'll have books and pictures and postcards all about dogs. And muzzles and blankets and dog-baskets and dog-biscuits, and things like that for real dogs."

"And china ornaments," said Kitty; "they're very often dogs, you know."

"Then there's the Fruit Tree," went on Miss Merington. "Not any one kind of fruit, you know, but all kinds. And under that will be sold fresh fruits, canned and preserved fruits, fruit pies, fruit cake, candied fruits, dried fruits—oh, you'll see for yourself what variety of fun it will make. And, of course, some of the allusions are jokes. The Fir Tree will sell furs."

"Oho!" laughed King; "sealskin coats and buffalo robes?"

"Well, perhaps not such expensive articles; but fur caps and mittens; and Teddy Bears, and toy-animals. Then there's the Evergreen Tree; of course, everything sold from that must be green. That's easy, you see, and yet it will be a beautiful tree."

"Which tree shall I be under?" asked Miss Larkin, eager to learn her appointed place.

"You may have the Evergreen, if you like. As I say, there's wide scope for choice of articles to sell."

"I'd like that very much," said Miss Larkin. "King and Kitty will be my helpers, and I'm sure we can get lots of green things ready for the bazaar."

"I'm sure you can," agreed Miss Merington. "And your tree will be easy to get, too. Just any kind of an evergreen tree will do."

"A Christmas tree," said King; "I'll ask Thomas to cut one in the woods for us."

"Yes, do. Some of the trees are much harder to manage. Many of them will have to be covered entirely with paper foliage."

"How about our tree—the Orange Tree?" asked Delight.

"Well, you see, our tree takes the place of what is usually known at fairs as the grab-bag or fish pond. We will make lots of oranges in this way. Take some little article that can be sold for five or ten cents, wrap it in cotton until it forms a ball the size of an orange, and then cover it with orange-colored crêpe paper. Tie it at the top with a narrow green ribbon, and hang it on the tree. Of course, the customer, buying an orange, takes his chance on what he will find inside it."

"Oh, that will be lots of fun," said Marjorie. "I can make little pincushions and sachet bags."

"Yes," said Delight, "and I can make little stamp-cases and tiny picture frames, and lots of things."

"And we can buy things," went on Midget. "Spools of cotton, and celluloid thimbles, and little bits of toys and dolls. Oh, can't we begin this afternoon?"

Miss Merington smiled at the enthusiasm of her young assistants.

"You may, if you choose," she said: "I must go now, but, of course, I'll see you again soon about our plans. Just go on and make all the oranges you can. I've brought you one, for a sample."

Miss Merington gave Marjorie a paper and cotton orange, which was so neatly made that it looked almost like a real one.

"Make them carefully," she advised, "for the whole tree will be spoiled if the fruit is ragged or badly shaped."

"What kind of a tree will you have, Miss Merington?" asked Marjorie.

"Fortunately, I'll have the real thing," was the answer. "A friend of mine, who has a large orange tree in his conservatory, is willing to lend it to me. It is in a very large tub, and it will be difficult to move it, but I think we can manage it. Then I shall have sprays of white orange blossoms made of paper, on it, and also our yellow fruit. Of course, we hope to sell many more oranges than would fill the tree, so we'll have a crate full, also, and sell them out of that, as well as from the tree."

"Do we sell anything else except the oranges we make?" asked Delight.

"Yes; I'd like to have a small stand, with a few other things, say, orange marmalade, and candied orange-peel, and such things."

"And shall we dress in orange-color?" asked Midget.

"Why, I hadn't thought of that, but it would be very pretty."

"I'll help you," said Miss Larkin. "I'll have a dress made of orange-colored cheesecloth for Marjorie, and I'm sure Delight's mother will let her have one, too."

"Oh, do," said Miss Merington. "I have a gown of orange chiffon and black velvet, so we will all be appropriately dressed."

"And we'll wear green," went on Miss Larkin. "I'll have green clothes made for King and Kitty, and I have a green silk already, myself."

"Ho!" laughed King, "I'd look fine in a green rig, wouldn't I!"

"Yes, you would," declared Kitty. "You'd look like a hunter or Robin Hood or somebody like that. It would be lovely."

"So it would," said Miss Merington. "You are very kind, Miss Larkin, to go to so much trouble."

"Oh, I like it. I'll get in a dressmaker for a few days, and she'll soon fix up the children's costumes. Cheesecloth for the girls, and paper muslin for King. They'll look fine, and not cost much, either."

"I do think, Larky," said Midge, after Miss Merington had gone, "that our trees will be the prettiest in the room."

"I don't know, child. She didn't tell us about all of them. But we'll fix ours up as well as we can. Delight, ask your mother to let you have your orange frock made over here, with Marjorie's. It would be easier all round."

"Oh, she will, Miss Larky. She'll be glad to do it. She just hates to have a dressmaker in the house. And Miss Hart will help me make the oranges, I know."

"What can we make?" asked Kitty. "So many things are green, that it's hard to think of anything."

"Why, Kit," said her brother, "there's hardly anything we can't sell at our table. If you want to make fancy things, you can make 'em all green. If you want things to eat, there's apples and pickles, and little cakes with green icing, and green candies, and green peppers!"

"And books with green covers," supplemented Marjorie.

"That's good!" cried Kitty. "I love to paste scrap-books, and I've a lot of gay pictures saved up. I'll make scrap-books for children, with green covers."

"Be sure the children have green covers," said King. "Look at them well, before you let them buy the books."

"You make good jokes," said Kitty, looking patronizingly at her brother; "but what are you going to make for our Evergreen Tree?"

"That's so," said King. "There aren't many things a boy can make. I can cut out some jigsaw puzzles, but if they're all green, there won't be any picture."

"Yes," said Midget, "use those pictures that are nearly all forest and green trees. They're the hardest to do, too."

"All right; I'll do a couple of those, but what else can I do?"

"Dolls' furniture," suggested Kitty.

"Yes, that's fine, but I guess you don't know how much trouble it is to make the chairs stick together. Well, I'll do a set or two, and stain the wood green, and you girls can make green satin cushions for 'em."

"All right," said Kitty; "I'll help you with the cushions, and then you can help me with the scrap-books. And, King, we can paint things green—baskets, you know."

"Yes, and tin cans, and old tea-chests, and then tie ribbons on 'em! No, thank you, I won't do any of that kind of stuff."

"Well, but pretty little baskets would be all right," said Marjorie, laughing; "and flower pots, too."

"Oh, yes," said Delight; "little flower pots with just a hyacinth or a fern in them. Then paint the pot green, and there you are!"

"That isn't so worse," said King; "and I might make a few window boxes."

"Oh, they would be lovely!" exclaimed Miss Larkin. "They'd look so pretty under our tree. We could get a couple like those you have, and fill them, and I'm sure they'd sell well."

"I shall make some penwipers," said Kitty. "You just cut a leaf like a maple-leaf out of green leather or kid, and then cut two or three leaves just like it of green felt, and fasten them together at the stem."

"And make some little lamp-shades," said Delight; "I mean, candle-shades. They're lovely of green paper—Mother has some."

"I can't make them neatly enough," objected Kitty. "You girls make me some of those, and I'll make some orange candies for you. I'll cut you out some orange baskets, if you want me to—made out of the orange-skins, you know."

"Oh, yes," said Marjorie; "Kit does make those just lovely. And we'll fill them with orange cream candies. Let's all make things for each other."

"I shall make some green silk work-bags," said Miss Larkin, "and green sofa-pillows. And I'll buy some things, like green writing paper and envelopes. I can't abide colored stationery myself, but some people like it."

"And it will look pretty on your table," said Marjorie. "Miss Merington says we have a table to put our things on to sell, and hang them on our trees, too. Kit, you can trim dolls' hats— you're fine at that."

"Yes, indeed; and they'll be pretty of light straw or white muslin and lace, and green bows, or a little wreath of tiny green leaves."

"Or green feathers," added Delight. "I have some I'll give you, off my last summer's hat."

"Well, let's get to work, then," said Kitty, who was prompt of nature. "There are enough things in the house to begin on."

So they all scampered up to the playroom, and after cleaning off the big table, they brought out what contributions they could make to the general stock in trade.

There was plenty of crêpe paper left over from previous festivities, and Kitty found enough pretty scraps of silk and velvet to begin on her fancy-work at once. So, though they didn't finish many articles that afternoon, they planned a lot of things, and made lists of the materials they needed to buy next day.

After that the days flew by quickly enough.

Afternoons were devoted to making the pretty trifles, the store of which grew rapidly, with so many eager little fingers at work.

The dressmaker came, and under the supervision of Miss Larkin and Miss Hart, concocted dainty little costumes that were most pretty and becoming, though made of humble cheesecloth. King's garb was most effective, for his suit of dark-green shiny muslin was set off by gilt buttons and a real lace collar.

As Arbor Day came nearer, the children made delicious home-made candies, all orange or green, and Ellen concocted wonderful cakes with pale-green icing, and with orange icing.

Then, besides the things they provided themselves, many goods were donated.

Rockwell was a generous community, and the householders and shopkeepers always responded liberally to requests for donations toward church or charity.

Mr. Gordon, who was a friend of Mr. Maynard's, invited the children to select wares from his shop to the extent of ten dollars, and such fun as they had!

Marjorie and Delight took a basketful of little trinkets for their "oranges," and King and Kitty were quite bewildered at the number of attractive green things they found.

Miss Larkin spent her money and her time both freely, and was voted the hardest worker in the whole bazaar.

She bought the window boxes, and had them prettily filled, and she bought, also, a number of ferns and small palms in green pots.

"I'm so glad I happened to be here just at this time," she said, "for I love an occasion of this sort, and I almost never get a chance to be in one."

CHAPTER XVIII
THE ARBOR DAY FESTIVAL
Arbor Day was the most beautiful day you ever saw. Not too warm, or too cool, or too wet, or too dry, or too cloudy, or too bright—but just perfect in every way. The festival was to be held both afternoon and evening, and Miss Larkin told the children they might go at two o'clock, when it opened, and stay until nine at night.

Of course, this meant they would eat their supper there, which was a satisfactory arrangement to them all.

Marjorie and Delight had dresses just alike, of orange-colored cheesecloth, bordered with green leaves. The leaves had been added, because they were suggestive of trees, and also because they made the dresses more becoming. Indeed, the orange color suited Marjorie's dark eyes and curls better than it did Delight's fair hair and pink-and-white complexion; but the decoration of green leaves made Delight look like a sort of wood-nymph. The Maynard carriage took the two girls over first, before Miss Larkin and her aids went, and Miss Merington welcomed them warmly.

She had not desired their help in the arranging of her tree, so Marjorie and Delight had not seen the festival before at all.

As they entered the door, they stopped, enchanted.

Surely, the old Town Hall had never before responded so nobly to beautifying efforts. Across one end was a grape-vine, trained over a rustic pergola.

Here, young ladies, garbed as Italian peasants, served such refreshments as grape-juice, grape-sherbert, white grapes, grape-salad, grape-jelly, and preserved grapes. The little tables looked very tempting, and though the grape-vine and leaves were all artificial, the effect was very fine indeed.

The girls laughed heartily at the next "tree," for it was a pair-tree!

Suspended from its branches were pairs of all sorts of things: scissors, slippers, gloves, mittens, earrings, bracelets, cuffs—in fact, everything that comes in pairs seemed to be there. This tree was presided over by two young ladies who were twins, and as they were dressed exactly alike, they made a most pleasing "pair."

"Ho! look at that tall tree!" cried Marjorie, as they came to an affair that looked like a flagpole with a lot of palm-leaf fans at its top.

"Don't be disrespectful of my tree!" returned Flip Henderson, who was assisting his mother at this very tree. "This is a Date Palm, and I rigged it myself. Isn't it fine?"

The tree was picturesque, though comical, and a vivid imagination could think that it resembled a date palm from the tropics.

"What do you sell?" asked Delight; "dates?"

"Yes," replied Flip. "But not dates to eat. We have calendars, and diaries, and memorandum blocks, and year-books of the best authors. Want a few?"

"Not now," said Marjorie; "I've only two dollars to spend, and I want to see the other tables—trees, I mean—before I decide what I'll buy."

"And we must go on, and see the trees, so we can go to our own," said Delight.

Hand-in-hand, the two girls went round the room, looking at the novel sights.

In a grove of Rubber Trees, many sorts of rubber goods were sold.

Under a beautiful tree, loaded with cherry-blossoms, Japanese maidens dispensed tea, and sold fans and paper parasols.

The Cork Tree was most amusing. Corks dangled from its branches, and stuck on the ends of its twigs. On its counter were sold bottles of perfume, of ink, of shoe dressing, of mucilage, everything, in fact, which could be corked in a bottle.

Also, there were some funny little curios and toys which had been cleverly carved out of cork, and some grotesque dolls with cork faces.

Under the Pine Tree were many things of wood. Matches, skewers, and kitchen implements, as well as picture frames, book-racks, and carved wooden boxes. Not all of pinewood, perhaps, but much latitude was allowed in this market. Here, too, were pillows of pretty silks, filled with balsam of pine, and little trinkets made of pine cones or pine needles.

A funny tree was the Weeping Willow. It was cleverly contrived, and looked almost like a real willow tree. Beneath it was a sale of nothing but handkerchiefs and onions!

The two merry girls in charge of this pretended to be weeping as they sold their wares, and so funny were their lamentations that soon they had no wares to sell.

The Beech Tree had all sorts of seashore goods—shells, coral, postcards of watering places, little pails and shovels—all reminiscent of the beach.

The Ash Tree was, of course, the stand for cigars and ash trays, or other smokers' utensils.

The candy was sold in a sugar-cane plantation, and refreshments were served in a thicket of trees called the Peach Orchard, because the pretty waitresses were said to be "Peaches!"

Altogether, it was a beautiful scene, and after a walk round it all, Marjorie and Delight reported at Miss Merington's Orange Tree.

This was one of the prettiest, for the tree was a real one, and large enough to present a fine appearance.

It was loaded with orange blossoms and with the "oranges" that the girls had made. There was also a crate of the paper oranges to sell from and, too, there was a crate of real oranges to be sold.

Then all sorts of orangey things that were good to eat, and orange-colored fancy articles beside.

Miss Merington had brought lovely dolls dressed in orange color, beautiful silk college flags, and cushions representing the college that sports that color, books bound in orange, and orange-colored fans and scarfs. Miss Merington, herself, looked lovely in her orange gown, and she told Marjorie and Delight that they were the most attractive things under her tree.

Marjorie had had a brilliant idea for their tree, and she told Miss Merington that she would attend to it all herself, and surprise her. The idea was to serve orangeade.

She had brought from home her mother's pretty little glass cups, and the way she proposed to exhibit the orangeade was the novelty. With Thomas' help she had taken a large cube of ice, and hollowed out the centre, until it was a sort of square tub.

She had done this by heating a tin bread-pan very hot, and melting out the inner portion of the ice.

Though she had never seen this done, and had only read about it in a magazine, the experiment proved successful, and the ice receptacle was like a large square tub of glass.

Thomas brought it over in triumph, and it was set in place on a gridiron concealed by a bed of green leaves. These leaves also concealed a big pan which was to catch the water as the ice melted from the warmth of the room.

But the sides and bottom of the ice bowl were about four inches thick, so it was bound to last for several hours, anyway.

"How are you getting on?" said King, coming along, as Midget arranged the glasses prettily on a tray.

"Fine! The ice well is great! See how nice it looks. Thomas has gone back home for the orangeade. Ellen made it, so it's sure to be good."

"You're all right, Mopsy. Delight, you look fine. Now I must go back to my Evergreen Tree. Come and see us when you can. We look pretty gorgeous, I can tell you."

King went off, and then Thomas came with the orangeade in a large pail.

"Put in about half, Thomas," said Midget, "and set the rest away till later."

"Yes, Miss Marjorie," he said, and Miss Merington looked on approvingly as the rich yellow liquid was poured into the clear ice tank. Ellen had added thin slices of orange, and some red cherries, and the compound looked most delectable.

Miss Merington showed Thomas where to store the rest of the orangeade, and then bade him look round the room and enjoy the gay scene.

The customers had begun to come now, and Marjorie and Delight were kept busy selling oranges to children who were eager to see what treasures would come out of the yellow prize packages they bought.

Great laughter ensued when a boy found he had purchased a doll, or a girl was rewarded with a tin whistle, but surprises like these were expected, and were part of the game.

Finally, some ladies and gentlemen sauntered by, and paused by Marjorie's table, saying they would take orangeade.

Taking up the silver soup ladle which she had brought for that purpose, Midget turned to the ice well to fill the glasses.

To her amazement, there was not a drop of orangeade in the well.

She could not believe her eyes! Had Delight sold it all when she wasn't looking? No, the dainty glasses that she had set on the tray herself had not been used. Where could the orangeade be? She had seen Thomas pour it in, not twenty minutes before, and now it was all gone! A few bits of orange and a few cherries lay in the bottom of the big ice bowl, but not enough orangeade to fill one glass.

Greatly embarrassed, Marjorie turned to her would-be customers, and asked them to wait a moment.

"Well, you are doing a rushing business," remarked the young man who had ordered the orangeade. "Used up all that tank full already! Why, it must hold two gallons."

Marjorie beckoned across the room for King to come to her assistance.

"The orangeade's all gone," she whispered to him. "Won't you get the pail from that cupboard where Thomas put it, and pour out some more?"

"Sure," said her brother; "how'd you sell it so quick?"

"I didn't sell it; I don't know who did. But never mind, get some more—quick."

"All right," said King, and in a few moments he brought the big pail and poured half its contents into the ice-bowl.

Meantime, Marjorie, turning to the guests, asked them to be patient a moment, and then she would serve them.

As King walked away with the pail, Midge again took up her ladle.

"Now," she said, smiling prettily, "I'll give you some orangeade."

"It's sure to be good and cold, served from that ice punch-bowl," said the young man.

"Yes, indeed," returned Marjorie, her voice betokening her pride in her clever achievement.

She turned to the ice-bowl, and there was not a drop of orangeade in it!

"King is playing a joke on me," she thought to herself, and her cheeks flushed with indignation that he should be guilty of such an ill-timed jest.

"King," she called, for he was crossing the room, "bring back that pail!"

"Whew!" he cried, turning back, "not sold out again!"

"You didn't put any in here!"

"I did so; I poured in three or four quarts."

"Well, where is it? This ice thing is empty."

"What! Why, so it is! Now, watch, I'll pour in some more."

He emptied the pail into the ice-bowl, and they both watched what happened. It disappeared almost as fast as he had poured it in.

"The old thing leaks!" cried King, going off into a burst of laughter. "Oh, Mopsy, Midget, you're a smart one!"

"Well, what makes it leak? Do you suppose anybody bored a hole in the ice?"

"No; they didn't have to! It's full of holes; look at it!"

Sure enough, the ice that formed the bottom of the receptacle showed a dozen or more good-sized holes. Though the slab was fully four inches thick, the holes went straight through, as if driven there with an auger.

The bits of orange and the cherries remained, but the orangeade had drained right through, and was now in the pan below that had been placed there to catch the melting ice.

"Oh, Mops! what a joke!" cried King, still doubled up with laughter.

"But who put the holes there? How did they get there?" persisted Marjorie.

"Why, ice is often that way. I s'pose air makes the holes; it bubbles up as the ice freezes. Sometimes there are so many holes that it's as porous as a sponge. And every time we pour the stuff in, it goes right through."

Much crestfallen, Marjorie turned again to the people who were patiently waiting for their order to be served.

"I'm sorry," she said, blushing rosily, "but I can't give you orangeade—because I haven't any left."

"What, what!" cried the young man, teasingly; "why, I just saw several quarts poured into that ice washtub there!"

"Yes," said Marjorie, "but it poured itself out again. You see, that's a beautiful ice-tub—but it leaks."

"It needs the plumber," said King, coming to his sister's rescue. "Just a leak in the pipes, somewhere. Sorry not to give you any orangeade, but we can only offer you these delicious paper oranges instead."

The young man laughed, and bought paper oranges for his party instead of the refreshment they had expected.

They didn't care, of course, for buyers at a bazaar are always good-natured, but Marjorie was greatly chagrined that her clever contrivance had failed.

"No matter," said Miss Merington, who had been occupied on the other side of the tree, and only heard about the mishap after it was all over; "no matter; it was a good enough scheme, but it fell through."

"It was good orangeade, but it fell through, too," laughed King. "Now I must skip. Don't you care, Midget, sell oranges and look happy."

This was good advice, and Midget acted on it.

"I'm glad it didn't work right," said Delight; "for it's messy stuff, anyway. I like better to sell paper things—they aren't sticky."

Delight had a rooted aversion to any thing sticky or untidy, but Marjorie was not so "fussy particular," as she phrased it. However, there were plenty of other things to sell, so Miss Merington called an attendant to take away the ice affair, as it was only in the way. Sure enough, as he lifted off the heavy block of ice, in the tub below could be seen all of Ellen's carefully prepared orangeade.

"It does seem a pity," said Midget, "but, as you say, Delight, it is sticky, and I'm glad to get it out of the way. Now, I'm going over to see King's tree."

Of course, Marjorie and Delight couldn't both leave their Orange Tree at once, so they took turns in going out on little excursions round the room.

Miss Larkin's tree was a beautiful, finely-shaped evergreen, and would have made a good Christmas tree. But it had no resemblance to a Christmas tree, for it was hung with green fans, parasols, aprons, motor veils, bags, sofa-pillows, and even some green hats, that a generous milliner had donated. Miss Larkin, herself, looking very fine in her green silk gown, was smiling and beaming at her customers, and incidentally making a great many sales.

King and Kitty were laughing over the joke of Midget's orangeade, but Miss Larkin regretted that so much money had been lost from the funds.

"Oh, pshaw, Larky," said King; "it wouldn't have amounted to very much, anyway."

"And, perhaps, if we had sold it, we might have broken some of those pretty glass cups of Mother's," said Midget, who always found the bright side.

"Well, then I'm glad it leaked away," said Kitty; "for I was afraid all the time you'd break those, and Mother's awfully fond of them."

"I know it," said Mopsy. "I'm going to tell her I took them, but I'll never do it again."

CHAPTER XIX
THE CONTEST
At six o'clock, Miss Larkin summoned the Maynards to supper. Delight, of course, accompanied them, and being in hospitable mood, Miss Larkin bade the younger Maynards invite Dorothy and Flip.

So it was a real Jinks Club feast, and a gay time they had. Substitutes had been put in their places at the trees, so they had no need to hurry.

"Have you heard about the contest, Mops?" said King, as he blissfully ate his chicken-salad, a luxury not often bestowed upon the Maynard children.

"No; what is it?"

"Why, Mr. Abercrombie has arranged a sort of game, something like a spelling match, only you guess trees instead of spelling words."

"Can anybody be in it?" asked Delight, who was fond of guessing games.

"Yes, if you pay a quarter. Let's all enter; will you, Miss Larkin?"

"No, King; I can't guess riddles—never could. But I'll look after our tree while you go to the contest—or whatever you call it."

"Of course, we won't get the prizes," said Kitty, "for I s'pose the grown-up people will guess better than we do. But it'll be fun to try."

Mr. Abercrombie was a genial old gentleman, beloved by everybody in the town. He was both rich and generous, so at a public fair or bazaar he was always expected to do his share, and more, too, and these expectations were always realized.

As he passed by the Maynards' supper table, he stopped to pat Marjorie on the head.

"Well, my little orange maiden," he said, "you look so like an orange, I think I shall squeeze you."

Marjorie smiled at him gaily, and he squeezed her plump arm as he said:

"Are you going to guess trees with us, this evening?"

"I'd like to," said Midge, "but I only know our common trees. I don't know about tropical or foreign trees."

"Well, the quizzes are pretty hard," admitted Mr. Abercrombie, "but you'd better have a try at it. I hope you'll all try," he added, genially; "the more, the merrier."

He passed on, and the Jinks Club resumed their supper.

"I wish Father and Mother were here," said Marjorie, as she looked round on the pretty scene. "I know we'll never have such a lovely show in town again."

"Well, they're seeing trees down South to beat these," said King.

"And anyway," said Kitty, "they'll be home next week, and we can tell them all about it."

"My! but I'm glad they're coming," said Marjorie; "seems to me I miss Mother more every day."

"Oh, Marjorie," cried Miss Larkin; "haven't I looked after you pretty well?"

"Yes, indeed, Larky, dear, you have. But, of course, you're not Mother, and somehow it does make a difference. I hope you'll stay a while after she gets home, and then we'll have you both."

"Perhaps," said Miss Larkin, smiling; "and now, if you've finished your ice cream, let's go back to our trees."

After Marjorie was again at her stand, selling oranges, Mr. Abercrombie came strolling by.

"Well, my orange maiden," he said, "I think I must patronize your very attractive tree. No, I don't care for grab-bag prizes. I'll take some jars of orange marmalade. You know, we must take the bitter with the sweet."

Marjorie liked the merry old gentleman, and to amuse him, she told him the story of her orangeade and the leaky ice-tub.

He laughed heartily. "Well, well," he exclaimed, "that was too bad, that was too bad! I suppose you felt terribly chagrined, eh?"

"Yes, I did," Marjorie admitted, "but, you know, we must take the bitter with the sweet."

"Good girl, good girl, to learn a lesson so quickly. Now, let me see; I'll buy some of these college traps. I have a grandson in Princeton, and he'll be glad to have them for his room. There, I'll take that, and that, and that. Now, if you'll make me out my orange bill, I'll pay you."

On a square of orange-colored paper, Marjorie wrote neatly the articles he had bought, and their prices. She added it correctly, and presented it with a business-like air.

"Well done, well done, little orange girl. And so I owe you nine sixty-five. Quite a big orange bill. But I'll make it ten dollars, if you can tell me of the greatest Orange Bill ever known."

Marjorie thought hard. She had been afraid this quizzical old gentleman would ask her some question that she couldn't answer. She thought of great shiploads of oranges coming up from the South, but she knew nothing about the price of them.

"No, sir," she said, finally, with a little sigh; "I don't believe I can tell you."

"Well, well, I'll give you the ten, all the same, for the good of the cause. And the Bill I have in mind was William of Orange."

"Oh!" said Marjorie, laughing; "well, even if I had thought of him, I couldn't tell you much about him. But I'll know more of him next week!"

"How's that? Does he come next in your history lesson?"

"No, sir; but in my school, we can have any lesson we want. If I ask Miss Hart to make a lesson on William of Orange, she will."

"Bless my soul! That's a fine school! And can all the pupils order subjects that please their fancy?"

"Well, you see," said Midget, with her eyes twinkling, "there are only two pupils. Here's the other."

She turned and drew Delight toward her.

113

"Oh, yes, another little Orangette. Well, you must be a fine class, you two. Now, see to it that you learn about William of Orange, and next year, if we have a bazaar, you can tell me all about him. I hope your memories are long enough for that."

"Oh, yes," said Marjorie. "I remember, at the bazaar last winter, you taught me some spelling."

"Why, you little wiseacre! You'll have too much book-learning, if you're not careful! Well, try the guessing contest this evening, and see how you make out at that!"

Mr. Abercrombie went away, and Delight said:

"Isn't he a pleasant old gentleman? But he twinkles his eyes so, he makes me jump."

"He likes to tease," said Marjorie, "but he's awfully generous. I expect he buys more than any one else at the fair."

"Hasn't he any people of his own?"

"Not that live with him. He lives all alone in a great big house. His wife is dead, and he has some grandchildren, but I don't know where they live. He's a kind man, anyway."

At eight o'clock the contest began. It was conducted like an old-fashioned spelling match— that is, two captains were selected, who chose sides.

Mr. Henderson was one captain, and Miss Merington was the other.

These two chose alternately until all who had entered the contest were ranged in two long rows, and the rest of the people looked on with great interest.

Mr. Abercrombie conducted the game, and as he walked up and down between the two rows, he caught sight of Marjorie's eager little face, and gave her an encouraging nod and smile.

Midget had been chosen on Miss Merington's side, and though she was sure she could not win the prize herself, she hoped she could at least help her captain to win it.

"This is the plan of our contest," announced Mr. Abercrombie, for few of them had ever seen the game before: "I will ask a question of Mr. Henderson, then of Miss Merington, then of the next one on Mr. Henderson's side, then of the next one on the other side; and so on down the two lines. Whoever answers a question correctly, remains in the game. Whoever does not do so, must be scored against, and the question passed on to the next. After three scorings, the contestant must drop out of line. The winner, of course, is the one who remains to the last. First, I will ask of Mr. Henderson, 'What tree do we give to our friends when we meet?'"

"Palm," answered Mr. Henderson, promptly, and everybody applauded.

Then Mr. Abercrombie asked of Miss Merington, "What is the housewife's tree?"

"Broom," she replied, for it had been explained that the answer need not necessarily be a tree, but a bush, or tall plant of any kind.

Marjorie's courage began to fail her. She liked puzzles, but these were pretty hard ones. However, the next ones were a little easier.

"Where do the ships land?" was readily answered "Beech," and "What is the dandified tree?" was "Spruce."

Delight had an easy one. She was asked, "What tree is most warmly clad?" and she said, "Fir" at once.

Other questions were asked, some were missed, and some answered correctly, and then King covered himself with glory by replying "Peach" to "What is the tell-tale tree?"

Nearer and nearer Marjorie's turn came.

At last, Mr. Abercrombie looked at her and said, "What is the historian's tree?"

Marjorie breathed a sigh of relief. She was safe for this round, anyway, and she said, "Date," with a smiling face. Then she listened, as the questions went round again.

Many missed this time, and it was a second scoring for some.

Again Marjorie had good luck.

"What tree is found in a bottle?" was the question.

She hesitated a moment, for she had hazy visions of tiny trees growing in bottles, then her wits returned like a flash, and she said, "Cork," which was right.

But she thought to herself, "I'm sure I should have forgotten that cork comes from a tree, if I hadn't seen the Cork Tree here to-night."

However, that might be equally the case with all the others, so it was perfectly fair.

That time, Delight had a hard one and missed it. The question, "What tree invites you to travel?" was too difficult for her.

It was passed from one to another, until a man answered, "O range," but he laughingly admitted he had heard it before.

"I'm glad I didn't get that question," thought Marjorie, for not even her orange frock would have helped her to guess that.

And so the game went on. Several dropped out on the third round, and after the fourth round, only about a dozen were left standing.

The two captains were still at the heads of their lines, and Marjorie and King had each missed only once; but the other Jinksies were all scored three times and out.

"What tree was an Egyptian plague?" asked the director.

"Locust," promptly replied Miss Merington, who hadn't missed yet.

"What tree destroyed Pompeii?" came next.

It was missed and passed on again and again, for nobody could guess it.

Midget and King both shook their heads, and this gave them each their second bad score.

It came round to the leaders, and as they both missed, it gave Mr. Henderson his third score, and put him out, but gave Miss Merington only her first score for missing.

As no one could guess it, the answer was told, "Mountain Ash."

Everybody agreed it was easy, after all, and the game went on with the few valiant strugglers that were left.

King couldn't think of "Elder" as an answer to, "What must everybody become before he gets old?" So he went ruefully to his seat.

On and on went the questions, until, at last, only Miss Merington and Marjorie were standing.

Marjorie had two bad marks, and Miss Merington only one, but the fact that Midget was still there at all, was due to the fact that most of her questions had chanced to be easy ones. There had been many given out that she couldn't answer, but they hadn't happened to come to her.

But these are the fortunes of war, and Marjorie was glad she had escaped so well.

After several that they guessed correctly, Mr. Abercrombie said, "What is the most kissable tree?"

It was Marjorie's turn, and as the question fell on her ears, an answer popped into her mind.

But she hesitated about saying it. She didn't think it was the right answer, and yet she couldn't think of any other.

But if she said she didn't know, she would get her third score, and have to admit herself vanquished.

Miss Merington smiled at her pleasantly, Mr. Abercrombie waited patiently, King and Kitty were looking at her anxiously. Why did she hesitate? they thought.

For Marjorie didn't look as if she didn't know the answer, she only seemed unwilling to tell it.

"Come, come, little orange girl," said Mr. Abercrombie, most kindly; "that's not a hard one. You can guess it, can't you?"

Still Marjorie said nothing.

"I'm sure that's the answer," she said to herself; "and yet suppose it shouldn't be!"

Then she thought she'd say she didn't know, and let Miss Merington get the prize. Then her conscience told her it would be wrong to say she didn't know, when she did know.

"Now, then, orange maiden," went on the kind voice, "here's your last chance. What's the most kissable tree?"

Finding that she must speak it, Marjorie blushed a little, but said in a clear voice, "Yew!"

Such a shout of laughter as went up from everybody! Mr. Abercrombie laughed until he was red in the face, and his huge form shook from side to side.

Of course, Midget was terribly embarrassed, and wished she could sink through the door, but Miss Merington took her hand and smiled at her sweetly, as she whispered, "Be plucky! Smile, yourself, you haven't said anything wrong!"

So Marjorie stopped trembling, and smiled a little; then she saw King and Flip fairly choking with glee, and she realized that her answer was wrong after all.

"I'm more than sorry," said Mr. Abercrombie, after the fun had subsided a little, "that I can't accept that answer! But I have to go by the card, and another answer is given here. So I shall have to pass the question, but I assure you, little orange girl, that I greatly prefer your answer to the one here given. Miss Merington, can you guess it?"

"Tulip tree," said Miss Merington, and Marjorie opened her eyes wide.

"I never heard of that tree," she said.

"Then you were very clever to guess as you did," declared Mr. Abercrombie. "Technically, you score your third error, and Miss Merington wins the prize; but in my unofficial capacity, I hold that you guessed correctly, and I shall beg the honor of bestowing upon you a prize also."

The old-time courtliness of Mr. Abercrombie's manner was quite a balm to Marjorie's disturbed spirit, and she turned to congratulate her captain on winning the beautiful prize.

It was a fine edition of Browning's Poems, and it pleased Miss Merington very much.

"It's just right for the lady who won it," commented Mr. Abercrombie, "but not at all appropriate for an orange girl of twelve. Now, you come with me, and we'll find the second prize right here and now."

He offered his arm as formally as if to a duchess, and in obedience to Miss Merington's smile and nod, Marjorie walked away with him.

He paused at the book stall, which was a somewhat ungainly old tree trunk, bearing the legend, "The Tree of Knowledge."

Beneath it on a table lay the books, under a sign, "Nothing but Leaves."

Mr. Abercrombie selected a fine edition of Longfellow's Poems, and inscribed Marjorie's name and the date on the flyleaf.

Beneath it he wrote:

"From one who appreciates Yew," and presented it in a flourishing fashion.

Midget had now entirely regained her composure, and she thanked him politely and prettily, and then ran away to join Miss Merington and Delight.

CHAPTER XX
A SPRING RAMBLE
"Only think!" cried Marjorie, as she sprang out of bed, "Father and Mother are coming home to-day!"

"Hooray!" cried Kitty, tumbling out of her bed at the joyful reminder. "Won't I be glad to see them, though! Aren't we going to celebrate?"

"Not any regular celebration. It'll be fun enough just to see them, and hear them tell about their trip."

"Yes, indeed; so it will. And, of course, we'll have ice cream."

"Oh, of course; I told Ellen that, yesterday."

A little later, two trim and tidy little Maynard girls went downstairs to the cheerful dining-room.

"Hello-morning!" cried King, meeting them on the landing. "Going to school to-day, Mops?"

"Yes, of course; why not?"

"Oh, I thought as Mother's coming home, we might take a holiday."

"No, I don't want to. They don't come till afternoon, you know, and if I hung round here all day, I'd just die waiting for 'em. Going to school will fill up the morning, anyway."

"That's so; say we go, then. Hello, Rosy Posy; did I 'most upset you?"

The four danced into the dining-room, where Miss Larkin and breakfast awaited them.

"I do think," said Midget, as she ate her cereal, "that, considering we're Maynards, we have behaved pretty well since Mother's been away."

"Sure we have!" agreed King; "if I get much better, I'll spoil."

"I'm spoiling for some mischief, as it is," said Marjorie, with dancing eyes.

"Oh, Mops," begged Kitty, "don't cut up any jinks before Mother gets home."

"Well, I won't," said Mops, who didn't mean her speech as seriously as Kitty took it; "but after she gets home, I'm going to cut up the biggest jink I can think of."

"Are you, really?" said Miss Larkin, with such a horrified expression that the three children could not help giggling.

"I dunno, Larky," said Midge, teasingly. "P'raps I will, and p'raps I won't. But I'll promise to be good as pie till Mother does come; only it seems as if to-day will be a hundred years long."

However, the morning passed rapidly enough to three Maynards, and it was not until after luncheon that they grew restless again.

"Oh, deary, deary me!" sighed Marjorie. "They can't come until five o'clock, and now it's only two. We can't dress up for them until about four—'cause there's no use dressing sooner, and getting all messy. Let's do something or go somewhere."

Miss Larkin hastily offered a suggestion. She well knew that when Midget grew restless and impatient, mischief was pretty likely to ensue.

"Let's go and weed the flower boxes," she said.

"They're spick and span now," said Marjorie. "We've weeded them every day this week, and if we pull up anything more it'll have to be the flowers themselves. And we've watered them till they're most drownded."

"Drowned, my child," corrected King, with a schoolmaster air.

"I don't mean drowned—I mean drowned dead," declared Marjorie, triumphantly.

"Pooh, if you're drowned, you're sure to be dead," returned her brother.

"You've never been drowned, so how do you know?"

"Neither have you, so how do you know?"

"There, there, children, don't quarrel," said Miss Larkin, pleadingly.

"Oh, pshaw, that isn't quarreling," said Marjorie; "that's only cheerful conversation; isn't it, King?"

"Yep," he returned, smiling good-naturedly. "We Maynards never really quarrel, we just sort of squarrel, you know."

"That's sort of between quarreling and squabbling," observed Kitty.

"Right you are, Kit! You grow brighter every day, don't you?"

Kitty beamed at her brother's compliment, for she well knew King meant it as such.

"Let's play games," suggested Miss Larkin next. "Shall we play Parcheesi?"

"Too poky," said Midget. "I want to run and jump round. Let's go outdoors. Come with us, Miss Larkin, and take a walk?"

"Larky, Larky," chanted King, "let's go to the park-y, and walk till after dark-y."

"Walk till nearly dark-y," corrected Marjorie. "Oh, I'll tell you what we'll do; we'll take a spring ramble."

"What's that? Something like this?" and King jumped up, and tripped across the room with affected mincing gait.

"No; it's just a walk in the spring. But you call it a spring ramble, if you go off on the country paths, and pick some wild flowers, and wonder what the birds are."

"Sounds good to me," agreed King. "Come on, ladies. Only we mustn't stay too long."

So they set off, Miss Larkin, Rosy Posy, and all, for a spring ramble.

It proved to be just the thing to divert their attention, and though they didn't forget the expected arrival, they became greatly engrossed in the wonders they found.

Marjorie was leader, because Miss Hart had taken her and Delight on two spring rambles already, and she knew how to look for the tiny wild flowers, that scarce showed their blossoms as yet.

"Those are marshmallows," announced Marjorie, proud of her knowledge, as she pointed to some rather tall green stems, growing near the brook.

"Marshmallows! Huh!" cried King in disdain. "Marshmallows don't grow on reeds!"

"I don't mean the candy kind," protested Marjorie. "These are a pink flower—when the flowers come—and I know they're it, for Miss Hart told me so. I think they're in bud."

"Those aren't buds, they're last year's seedpods," said King.

"I don't think so, but let's go down and see. The principal thing you do on a spring ramble is learn things."

They were on a high bank, and the descent to the growing things down by the brook was rather steep, and very stony.

"I can't go down there," declared Miss Larkin. "You children go, if you like, and Baby and I will wait up here for you."

"No, we must all go," said Marjorie, who was in wilful mood to-day.

"Oh, come on, Larky, dear," wheedled King; "we'll all take hold of hands and scamper down, just as easy as ease!"

So the five joined hands, and when King had counted, "One, two, three! Go!" they ran down the slope.

But though the stony bank was treacherous, it was nothing compared to the trouble they found on the lower level.

The impetus gained on the steep slope sent them running rapidly forward, and they found themselves stumbling in mud and mire.

"Whew!" exclaimed King, as they were stopped at last by their own clogging footsteps; "who'd have thought this was soft mud? It looked hard enough!"

Miss Larkin looked utterly disgusted. She tried to take a step forward, failed, lost her balance, and fell over against Rosy Posy, upsetting the poor child entirely. But the youngest Maynard was not one of the crying sort, and she floundered about in the mud, smiling hopefully, as she said:

"Middy; King; pick up poor Wosy Posy!"

But Midget and King were so convulsed with laughter at the comical appearance of Miss Larkin, that Rosy Posy was unheeded for the moment, and the baby good-naturedly floundered on, getting muddier at every step.

"I can't get my feet out of this mire," said poor Miss Larkin; "it's like a quicksand."

"Is it?" inquired King, with great interest; "I always wondered what a quicksand was like. But I don't care for it much, myself," he added, looking ruefully at his own shoes, muddied all over, and, indeed, half sunk in the ground.

"How shall we get out, King?" asked Kitty. "I think this is a horrid place."

"Oh, we'll get out all right," answered King, cheerfully. "Here, this is the way to do it. Turn down these bushes, and walk on 'em, see?"

It was a good plan, only the bushes chanced to be brambly ones, and their hands were scratched and their clothes were torn in their struggle to get out of the mud.

King lifted Rosy Posy high, in an endeavor to get her over unharmed; but thinking it was all a fine game, the little one gave a wriggle of delight, and fell plump into the soft mud.

"Oh, you mud-turtle!" cried King. "Well, Rosy Posy, you're a sight now! But it's lucky you didn't fall into the bramble bush."

"And scratch out both your eyes," added Marjorie.

"Mine are about scratched out," said Kitty, plaintively.

"Try the other bush, Kit, and scratch 'em in again," proposed King, who was struggling manfully to carry his littlest sister and help Miss Larkin at the same time.

Well, after a time, they did get out, and were such a looking crowd as can scarcely be imagined!

But they were once more on firm pavement, and though terribly scratched up, were not seriously injured. It was a narrow escape, though, for the mire was deep, and the thorns were sharp, and a bad accident might have happened.

"You said you wanted to cut up jinks, Midget, and now you've done it!" said her brother.

"No more than the rest of you," returned Midget. "Larky looks just as Jinky as any of us."

They all turned to Miss Larkin, and then burst into laughter. She did look funny, with her hat awry, her hair out of place, a daub of mud on her cheek, and her skirts beplastered with sticky mire, and caught here and there with brambles. Somewhat to the children's surprise, she took the disaster humorously, too.

"I don't look a scrap worse than you four do," she said. "But I'm thankful there are no eyes really scratched out, and no arms or legs broken; nothing but torn clothes, and dirty hands and faces, all of which can be set right in an hour or so. Now let's scramble for home, and we're plenty of time to get in spick and span order before your father and mother come home."

"I'm glad it isn't later," said Marjorie. "Just think of their catching us looking like this!"

They went home by a back street, and fortunately met no one on the way.

As they entered their own gate, and walked up the driveway, Marjorie said:

"It reminds me of the night we walked up here with the Simpsons. Only, we're a worse-looking crowd than they were."

"We're a worse-looking crowd than anybody ever was anywhere," said King, with conviction. "Here, Rosy Posy, you walking mud-puddle, brother'll carry you up the steps."

Rosy Posy nestled her soft, muddy cheek against King's equally muddy one, for she dearly loved her big brother, and liked to have him carry her now and then.

Up the steps they went, and in at the front door, and there, in the hall, stood—Mr. and Mrs. Maynard!

"Oh, Mother!" cried Marjorie; "oh, Mother!"

"Oh, Midget!" was the response, and then, regardless of the muddiness of Midget, and the tidiness of Mrs. Maynard, the two little arms flew round the mother's neck, and Marjorie's kisses left visible evidence on her mother's pretty pink cheeks.

"It was nice of you to fix up like this to welcome us," said Mr. Maynard, who had Rosy Posy in his arm now, and Kitty clinging to his other side.

Then muddy Kingdon was folded in his mother's embrace, and then, somehow, everybody embraced everybody else, quite thoughtless of mud or scratches.

"But what's it all about?" went on Mr. Maynard. "I like it—oh, don't think I don't like it! but—it's a new style to me."

"I feel that I am responsible for the children," began Miss Larkin, and all at once Marjorie saw that Miss Larkin was painfully embarrassed at having seemingly neglected her charge.

"Not a bit of it!" declared Midget, flying to Miss Larkin's side, and embracing the muddy lady; "it isn't the least bit Larky's fault! Is it, King? We went for a spring ramble——"

"And you sprang in," interrupted her father.

"Yes, we did. And we didn't expect you so soon, and we thought we'd get cleaned up 'fore you came. But you came sooner than we 'spected, didn't you?"

"Yes; we caught an earlier train than I thought we could."

"Well," Marjorie went on, "I'm glad you did—awful glad—'cause it didn't seem's if I could wait for you another minute! But I'm sorry we look so 'sreputable—but we can soon get washed, you know—only, I just want to say it wasn't Larky's fault—not the leastest mite! She's done the best she could to take care of us Maynards, and make us behave. But nobody can make Maynards behave. Can they, Father?"

"No," said Mr. Maynard, with twinkling eyes, and a glance at his wife; "no, nobody can make Maynards behave—but Maynards!"

Note from the Editor

Odin's Library Classics strives to bring you unedited and unabridged works of classical literature. As such, this is the complete and unabridged version of the original English text unless noted. In some instances, obvious typographical errors have been corrected. This is done to preserve the original text as much as possible. The English language has evolved since the writing and some of the words appear in their original form, or at least the most commonly used form at the time. This is done to protect the original intent of the author. If at any time you are unsure of the meaning of a word, please do your research on the etymology of that word. It is important to preserve the history of the English language.

Taylor Anderson